THE
RETURN
OF BUDDY
BUSH

Also by Shelia P. Moses

The Legend of Buddy Bush
A National Book Award finalist
A Coretta Scott King Author Honor recipient

*I, Dred Scott: A Fictional Slave Narrative Based on
the Life and Legal Precedent of Dred Scott*

Margaret K. McElderry Books

THE
RETURN
OF BUDDY
BUSH

Shelia P. Moses

Margaret K. McElderry Books
New York   London   Toronto   Sydney

Margaret K. McElderry Books

An imprint of Simon & Schuster Children's Publishing Division

1230 Avenue of the Americas, New York, New York 10020

This book is a work of fiction. Any references to historical events,

real people, or real locales are used fictitiously. Other names, characters,

places, and incidents are products of the author's imagination, and any resemblance

to actual events or locales or persons, living or dead, is entirely coincidental.

The text for this book is set in Fairfield Light.

Manufactured in the United States of America

10 9 8 7 6 5 4 3 2 1

Library of Congress Cataloging-in-Publication Data

Moses, Shelia P.

The return of Buddy Bush / Shelia P. Moses.—1st ed.

p. cm.

Summary: Following her grandfather's death in rural North Carolina in 1947, twelve-year-old Pattie
Mae learns more about her family after reading her grandmother's collection of obituaries and
traveling to Harlem, New York, to find her uncle Buddy, who has escaped from the Ku Klux Klan.

ISBN-13: 978-0-689-87431-4

ISBN-10: 0-689-87431-6 (hardcover)

[1. Family—Fiction. 2. African Americans—Fiction. 3. Race relations—Fiction.] I. Title.

PZ7.M8475Ob 2006

[Fic]—dc22

2004020503

FIRST
EDITION

I dedicate this book to my hero and high school principal,
Mr. William Spencer Creecy Jr., who departed from us on
August 5, 2005.

And to my four oldest siblings, Barbara, Daniel, Johnny, and Scarlett

If you call upon your ancestor's names, they shall hear you.
Therefore, they will never die.

CONTENTS

1

The Obituaries

*L*ord have mercy. My grandpa is dead. Dead and gone. Braxton Jones was his name. Today we had his funeral at Chapel Hill Baptist Church, right here in Rich Square. It was a long, sad funeral. Folks did some hollering and crying and I thought his best friend, Mr. Charlie, was going to have a nervous breakdown right there in the church. He was just hurt. His wife, Miss Doleebuck, never made a sound as she held Mr. Charlie's hand tight. So tight that his hand turned red. Red as a beet.

My grandma, Babe Jones, did some crying.

But not out loud. She cried inside with her proud self. Now my ma, Mer Sheals, just cried all she wanted to. Out loud! She was loud like the thunder and lightning outside the church window. It rained so hard the day they buried my grandpa. The ground was wet like my big sister BarJean's face. I believe she did the most crying. Her and my big brother Coy, who drove down from Harlem together in his new light blue Cadillac. Blue just like the one that my uncle Buddy Bush used to drive when he moved back down here from Harlem five years ago in 1942. Back down to Rehobeth Road where Grandma said he belonged. I bet she ain't saying that mess now. Don't nobody with good sense be saying it now. Everybody in Rich Square knows that Uncle Buddy should have stayed North. North of Baltimore, where colored men belong, so they can be men.

Grandma ain't saying nothing now because, you see, my uncle Buddy was not at the funeral. He ain't been around for a month. That is why Grandpa is dead. This ain't got nothing to do with the tumor on Grandpa's brain that the new colored doctor told us would kill him before the cotton bloom. See, the white folks killed Grandpa. No, they did not shoot him. They did not stab him. They did not try to hang him like they tried to hang my uncle Buddy. Grandpa died from a broken heart about my uncle Buddy and what the white folks did to him. Yep, the white folks worried Grandpa right to his grave because they ran Uncle Buddy off. Well, they didn't run him away. Uncle Buddy ran away on his own to stay alive. Had he stayed in these parts, he would be dead too. Dead as Grandpa. It's a shame and a disgrace how white folks treated my uncle. He ain't never done nothing to nobody but had a little white liquor every now and then. Ain't no law against that. But you know what? The white folks got him anyway.

All Uncle Buddy did was take me to the picture show one night in June after we were done eating catfish at Grandma's house just like we do every Friday night. We had such a nice drive into town. We ate ice cream while we waited for his date Miss Nora to get off work at the sewing factory right across the street from Myers Theater. What happened to Uncle Buddy that night was a shame 'fore God. What happened to our lives next was worse.

See, this white woman that passed Uncle Buddy on the sidewalk that night said he tried to rape her. I said she was a lie then and I say she is a lie now. Look-a-here, I saw the whole dag-gon thing and Uncle Buddy ain't tried to rape her nowhere. What really happened was Uncle Buddy did not do what Grandpa been telling him to do ever since he moved back to Rehobeth Road. Grandpa told him when you see white folks coming, just move over and let them pass. Uncle Buddy said, "To hell with them white folks." He said he would not move if they paid him.

He should have moved that night. He stood up so the white lady would walk past him, but he didn't move off of the sidewalk for her. So she went to the sheriff and told him her big lie and they arrested my uncle for nothing. Off they went to the jailhouse with Uncle Buddy. Me, they grabbed up like a rag doll and took me home to my folks on Jones Property.

A few weeks later, while Uncle Buddy was awaiting his trial, the Klan broke him out of jail and tried to hang him. Uncle Buddy is so much smarter than them white folks, because he jumped out of the boot of their car and hid in the swamp where the colored Masons found him and took him North. I tell you the other thing he did, he made it all the way north to Harlem. Well, that's where we think he is.

That was sure good for Uncle Buddy, but all the stress on my poor grandpa was just too much and that is why he's dead and I am sitting on the floor putting Grandpa's obituary in a wooden chest—the chest that Grandpa carved thirty years ago out of an old oak tree that fell after a tornado came through Rich Square in the middle of the night.

I ain't never gone in this chest before. Grandma said can't nobody on Jones Property go in this chest until you are twelve years old. On Rehobeth Road, everything happens when you twelve. You get baptized, you get your hair pressed for the very first time, and some girls even get their period. But if you are a Jones, you get to go in the old oak chest and put the obituary away after a Jones funeral.

So last year when my cousin June Bug drowned, Grandma would not let me put his obituary in the chest because I was only eleven back then. But Ma put it in right here. His cousin Willie's, on his daddy's side, obituary is here too. They both drowned on the same day and we had their funerals on the same day too.

Now here are both their dead folks' papers. Right on top. That's a sad sight. Under them two are so many obituaries that it would take me all day to count them. This is something else. I don't believe a person has died on Rehobeth Road, or all of Rich Square for that matter, that Grandma didn't save their obituary.

I can't believe that Grandma has saved all of those papers. It must be two hundred or more. Yep, I bet it's two hundred in here. Grandma even got the obituary from the twins, Big One and Little One's funeral. They was twelve when they got killed in a car accident coming from a stickball game. Grandma got Mary Lou's dead folks' paper too. That woman died because she was too fat. Four hundred pounds too fat.

I know I better close the chest up and get back out in the sitting room with all the folks who came to the funeral to say good-bye to Grandpa. I know my best friend, Chick-A-Boo, want me to come back in there with her. She been with me all evening. But she can't come in this room. This room and this chest are for folks with Jones blood only. So she is stuck in there with the gossiping folks from Rehobeth Road. Just listen at them. They just sitting around talking and eating up all the good cakes and pies that folks cooked for us. There ain't going to be a thing left when Toe Worm leave. Poor thing. We call him Toe Worm because his toes are so curled up that he don't hardly wear shoes. His real name is Pen Paul. Heck, I think I would rather be called Toe Worm. Whatever we call him, it don't stop Toe Worm from eating folks out of house and home. He done eat two helpings of food. Now he's working on Grandma's church friend Miss Thelma's lemon pie. Toe Worm is Miss Thelma's nephew on his ma side of the family.

I put the obituaries back in the chest and close it tight, just like it was when Grandma sent me in here.

Look at these folks just sitting around talking about Grandpa and how nice the funeral was. "Who in the world wrote the obituary? It was some kind of nice," Miss Ethel Mae say in between eating her third piece of chicken. She don't need to eat another piece because she is as big as a house already.

Ma rolls her eyes at Miss Ethel Mae before she open her mouth. "Ethel Mae, you know good and well I wrote that. You ask the same question after every funeral, like you don't know that when coloreds in Rich Square die, they folks come and get me to write they obituary."

Miss Ethel Mae just rolls her eyes back at Ma and bites her chicken again. Ma better leave that big woman alone. All she got to do is sit on

Ma, just like she sat on top of Miss Cathy when Miss Cathy was running her mouth at Miss Ethel Mae in the cotton field last year. If she does, I can't help Ma, because Miss Ethel Mae might sit on me, too. Ma said that only crazy folks fight all the time. I say that folks with good sense better keep they mouth closed. Tight!

You know, I really don't have time for all this grown folks' mess. I want them to take their tails home so that I can go back in that room and count some of them obituaries. Maybe I will take one from Grandpa's funeral and give it to Uncle Buddy when I see him. Lord knows when that will be.

While Ma and Miss Ethel Mae still rolling they eyes at each other I go on into the kitchen where Grandma is and wouldn't you know she is sitting in Grandpa's chair, next to the woodstove. I left Chick-A-Boo again, because she and her Ma should have enough sense to go home. I love her, but I am tired and I want to just be with people that got Jones blood.

"Grandma Babe, are you all right?"

"Child, Grandma is going to be fine. I just miss Braxton some kind of bad. I have lived with that man most of my life. I gave him five children and we buried two. And Buddy, he out there somewhere on the run for something he did not do. With all of that, Grandma is still all right."

Miss Doleebuck sitting in the kitchen too and she looking at me like I better go on about my twelve-year-old business. That's fine too, because I want her to leave Jones Property and go home. She been here all evening and I am tired. Most of all I want to get back in that chest before I go to sleep.

Finally, one by one, the folks leave Jones Property and head home. Mr. Charlie, Miss Doleebuck, and their children are the last to leave. Mr. Charlie and Miss Doleebuck got another boy up North somewhere, but he don't never come South of Baltimore. I know he's there, because I overheard Grandpa say so one night when I was testing a new mason jar up against the bedroom wall.

The other thing I know is that boy of theirs, Park Lee, ain't got good sense because he talk to himself all the time and he don't ever stop playing with that green yo-yo of his. Now, that would be fine if he wasn't thirty years old.

Anyway, they all gone now and I am glad. Chick-A-Boo is sad because she has to leave me. But I am happy to see her go. Miss Nora is leaving too. She is so upset about Grandpa dying and Uncle Buddy running off, but she said she will check on us from time to time. She still calls herself Uncle Buddy's girlfriend. If I was Miss Nora, I would get me a new boyfriend, just in case Uncle Buddy can't come back to these parts.

I take a peep in the kitchen again.

Grandma and Ma in there cleaning up. The women folks that were here earlier did some cleaning up for us after the funeral, but that ain't good enough for these women folks. Not the Jones women. They want the floors to be like dishes, clean enough to eat off of. While they scrubbing the walls, this is a good time for me to go back and look in the chest and to take a copy of Grandpa's obituary for Uncle Buddy. A good time for me to read about all them dead folks. Dead folks who use to live on Rehobeth Road and in Rich Square.

2

The Milkman

Ma and Grandma still in the kitchen wiping every corner.

The cups.

The plates.

The stove.

The floors.

Lord, they just wiping.

Ma is crying.

She need to clean the mirrors, too. Grandma covered every mirror in the house last week when Grandpa died. They were covered all week until we got home from the funeral. Grandma took all the covers off except the one in my back bedroom where my cousin, Collie, been sleeping. I guess she will uncover that mirror tonight. Covering the mirrors is a part of dying on Rehobeth Road. That's what the colored folks do around here. They believe it's bad luck to look at yourself when somebody dies. Uncle Buddy said that ain't so. But Uncle Buddy also said that he don't have to move off the sidewalk for the white folks and look where that got him with his hardheaded self.

Let me tell you how hardheaded Uncle Buddy really is. Ma said after his folks died and Grandma and Grandpa took him in he would sit in the kitchen every day and watch Grandma cook. One day when he was about my age, he said the stove did not look hot enough to cook the biscuits. Grandma told him to go about his business and the stove was fine. Guess what he did. He said, "No, it ain't hot," and touched the stove with his bare hand. Grandma and Grandpa tore his behind up. Ma said Uncle Buddy had a sore hand and a sore behind for a week. He's just hardheaded.

I love myself some Uncle Buddy, but I do have to talk to him about not believing in some of the stuff that the old folks on Rehobeth Road believe in. First Uncle Buddy said, "The young are strong, but the old know the way." Then he do not listen when he should. I ain't going to turn on Uncle Buddy for Grandma, but I just know Grandma can tell you some good stuff when she ain't fussing her little gray head off, and Grandpa ain't never told us nothing wrong. Never! You just got to listen and don't get mad. So mad that you get in trouble for not listening. Because Uncle Buddy did not listen, we here without our men folks. And Coy can't stay down here because Uncle Buddy got a hard head. Besides, Coy is going to marry that girl name Mary this November. She up in Harlem planning the wedding while Coy down here getting fussed at by the controlling women. Right now he and BarJean gone down Rehobeth Road, to the house where me and Ma live, to spend the night.

The old slave house. Uncle Buddy use to live in the slave house too.

Ma sisters, Aunt Louise and Aunt Rosie, so broke down from their trip down from Harlem and the funeral that they fast asleep in the room where Ma sleep when we stay here. Until they leave, me and Ma staying in the little bedroom off of the kitchen, because Collie sleeping in my room. Ma say they city folks and they need their own room so they can do as they please. Ma say they lazy and we got work to do. We do not have time to tiptoe around in the bedroom while they sleep late. She said we'll be fine in the other room until they leave. I do not care where they sleep; right now, I'm looking in the chest again. The dead folks' chest.

I stick my hand down in the chest to the very bottom. I'm almost scared to look at what I pull out. But I'm looking. This obituary is sixty years old. It is for a lady named Nicey Lewis. That would be Grandma's stepmomma. My grandma told me that her blood momma, Mae Fannie, died when she was born. Her daddy, George

Lewis, had to raise her by himself for a little while. Grandma said that she did not even have her ma's breast milk to drink, just milk from the cow.

Grandma said she was about two when her papa (my great-granddaddy), George Lewis, married this kind lady named Nicey Tann. That was her maiden name. Grandma said she was about ten before she realized that Grandma Nicey was not her real momma. It ain't nothing her kinfolks told her. They from Rich Square and everything is a secret around here until you grown. Even when you grown, I think you get a piece of news here and a piece of news there. That is why the mason jar is so important in my life. I ain't asking nothing. I will ease drop with my mason jar up against the walls until I get the truth.

Now, this is the truth. I ease dropped and learned about my grandma one day when she was talking to Miss Doleebuck. Grandma did not have much schooling because she had to stay home and work in the fields. But on the days when it was too cold to work, Grandma would walk to the schoolhouse up in town for a few hours. She said one day she was teasing a girl at school named Betty Sue about her half-pressed hair when Betty Sue just upped and got real mad and told Grandma all about herself.

"You think you is something special, don't you, Babe Lewis. Let me tell you how special you ain't. You don't even have a real momma. My momma said that your momma is dead and that lady you live with ain't your momma. Now how you like that, with your bow legs?"

Betty Sue laughed at Grandma and poor Grandma said she ran all the way home crying loud and acting crazy.

Great-Granddaddy Lewis was not home when she got there, but she told her Grandma Nicey what Betty Sue said. Grandma Nicey started to cry too and held her girl until her daddy got home from the cotton field around suppertime. That's when they told her about her real momma, Mae Fannie.

Mae Fannie got sick while she was giving birth

to Grandma. So sick that she took her last breath when Grandma took her first. Grandma don't know much else. She did say that Mae Fannie has a twin sister who is still living up in Baltimore and her name is Fannie Mae. She's about one hundred years old now and she is blind. She don't ever come to Rehobeth Road. But Grandma don't visit her either. Grandma said, "What does being blind have to do with sitting your behind on a train and coming down South? If she don't ever come to Rehobeth Road again, I will not go to Baltimore. Never."

Anyway, Grandma told Miss Doleebuck that after Betty Sue told her about her real mama, Grandma never talked to Betty Sue again. But it made her love Grandma Nicey even more for taking her and raising her like she was her own and all. That's probably the reason Grandma was so happy to raise Uncle Buddy, being that somebody that was not her momma raised her.

Grandma Nicey must have been some kind of woman. And I'm looking at her dead folks' paper right now. It is old and yellow, but I can read it.

Folded in her paper is George Lewis's dead folks' paper. It don't say much. Just stuff like he went to Chapel Hill Baptist Church and he was married twice. Grandma was his only child and all that. But no mention of a momma and daddy.

According to Uncle Buddy, Great-Granddaddy Lewis did not know his folks. They were slaves and sold away from each other when Great-Granddaddy Lewis was a baby. He was raised right here in Rich Square all his days. I don't know how he got to Rehobeth Road, or to Rich Square for that matter. I do know that when I am old enough I am going to go up to the county courthouse in Jackson and see what I can find out. My biology teacher, Miss Frances Clark, said that there is all kind of stuff about land and mommas and daddies up there. Maybe while I'm there I will look up something about my no-good daddy Silas Sheals's folks. He left Ma for another woman. On second thought, I don't care nothing about him or his folks. I'm a Jones to my bones and that's all to that. Mama said the man who loves you is your daddy.

So Grandpa and Uncle Buddy are my daddies and that's that. End of story.

But it would be something nice to find out more about Great-Granddaddy Lewis's folks. Well, maybe I don't want to know too much. See, Uncle Buddy said that a lot of folks around here got half-white great-grandparents. "Look at these people," he said one day when I ask him why Miss Doleebuck is so light skinned. "Some of these folks are just as yellow as a cake of butter."

He is right about that and I ain't that dark myself. Not like my best friend Chick-A-Boo. Surely she can't have no white blood. That is one black pretty child. Ain't no white folks able to be related to nobody that dark.

I believe if I look in this chest long enough I will find out who all my folks was. I believe I can even find out who Uncle Buddy's folks was. Don't nobody talk about Uncle Buddy's folks no more. Grandma and Grandpa raised him up after they died over in Rocky Mount in a tobacco barn accident. But if I find out something good, I am going to tell Uncle Buddy. If I find their obituaries, I am going to give them to him, because he did tell me that he didn't have much memory of them. Maybe there is something in the dead folks' paper that will help him to remember. Lord, I can't wait to get to Harlem to find him. Fixing on that Uncle Buddy is there, like folks is saying in the fields. They might be right. Might not!

After the funeral Ma said that I would be going back to Harlem with BarJean for a while. I am going to start packing come morning and I ain't telling nobody what I am putting in my suitcase. I'm taking short pants, two dresses, and the makeup that Miss Nora gave me last week. And I am going to take some of these obituaries and read them on the train while BarJean is sleeping. I know she is going to fall asleep before we leave Rocky Mount. Rocky Mount is where the train is leaving from. The train don't come through this little one-horse town.

Don't nothing come through here but the cotton man to buy all the cotton that we pick and the tobacco man come and buy all the tobacco we pick. Of course the big old milk truck come every day to pick up the milk from Mr. Bay's dairy that's across the road from Jones Property. I want to go over there so bad and see how Mr. Bay get the milk out of them big cans into that even bigger can on the back of the milkman's truck. But I can't go over there because Mr. Bay ain't that crazy about colored folks. Now he was nice to us when Uncle Buddy had to run away and he came to Grandpa's funeral. But he still don't want us on his land. When the white milkman comes, I run to the end of the path and put my thumb up and pull my arm down. That mean "hello" around here, and then he pulls this string in the roof of his truck and makes the horn blow real loud. Lord, that is so much fun to me. I think it's just knowing that the milkman ain't from around here that keeps my blood cooking on high. The license tag on the milkman's truck reads Virginia. I ain't never been to Virginia before and I just love knowing that I see someone from another state every day of my twelve-year-old life. I can hear him coming as soon as he turns off of Bryantown Road onto Rehobeth Road and that's when I start running to the end of the path. Me and my dog Hobo. If I am here on Jones Property, Grandpa's cat Hudson runs right behind us.

Last year I was here on Jones Property eating supper when the milkman came and the strangest thing happened.

"Grandma, please let me go thumb the milkman." I would not dare get up from eating supper without asking the woman of the house. That's the rule when I am here on Jones Property. I ask Grandma, not Ma, for permission to do whatever I think I am going to do. The reason I say "I think" is because you don't get to do a thing without a grown folks yes.

Grandma said yes because I asked in such a nice way. If I had just jumped up, she would had taken her cane and dragged me back to the table the way she did when I jumped up to meet Uncle Buddy when he was coming home from work one day. You have to see her punish us with her cane to believe it. She sticks it out with the hoop pointed toward you. Then she catch your leg, right at the knee with that hoop. Down you go! One day that woman is going to break somebody leg with that old cane.

That day, after she said, "Go on and thumb the milkman," I ran to the end of the road and waited. When the milkman got close, I threw my arm high in the air with my thumb up. I couldn't believe it. He didn't blow. I threw my thumb up again. He still didn't blow. That man saw me and did nothing. When he turned onto Bay's Property, I noticed that it was not the driver that comes every day. But they all know about the thumb. What was wrong with him? Mr. Bay's grandchildren were standing outside with their thumbs up too. When the milkman got in the driveway, he pulled his string twice for them. So he don't like colored folks either. That thing hurt me so bad I did not know what to do. I thought about that time Chick-A-Boo really hurt my feelings when she laughed at my run-down shoes. When I told Uncle Buddy about her laughing at me, he said, "Gal, you get your love at home."

So I ran back to Jones Property after the white milkman broke my heart because he didn't blow at me. I didn't go home to tell Grandpa. I went home to be loved. I didn't tell Grandma, because she probably would have walked right off of Jones Property onto Bay's Property and showed that driver how she can use her cane.

When I got in the kitchen, my folks were smiling at me. Grandpa said, "So the milkman pulled his string twice today."

"Yes, sir, he did."

I lied.

We ate our supper. I ain't thinking about that milkman.

I get my love right here on Jones Property.

3

The Packing

I'm going to miss my grandpa and having supper with him most nights of the week. Always on Friday. On Friday me and Ma leave our house and come here to Jones Property for our catfish supper.

I miss Uncle Buddy, too. Maybe when I go to Harlem and find my uncle, I can bring him home. Then he can be the man in the house. Now that Grandpa is dead, Uncle Buddy should be the man around Jones Property and the slave house. When I find Uncle Buddy, he will smile when he read Grandpa's obituary and the good stuff written about him. I want Uncle Buddy to see his name on the dead folks' paper. See, blood kin or not, his name is still put on this here obituary as Grandpa's son.

I tuck Grandpa's obituary in my pocket for Uncle Buddy right here, right now. I will come back for some more dead folks' papers before leaving for Harlem.

Out in the sitting room, Ma and Grandma going through Grandpa's things. They done almost wiped the wallpaper off the kitchen wall, they scrubbed it so hard. Now the controlling women talking about giving all Grandpa's clothes to Mr. Charlie. I don't know if I like that or not. But if they have to give them to anybody, Mr. Charlie is the person Grandpa would want to have his belongings. Grandpa had some nice things. The hats that Aunt Rosie brought him every time she came home from Harlem are still in the boxes. She even brought one when she came home for the funeral. Ma asked her why she brought a hat for Grandpa knowing he was dead. Her answer was sad. Sad like this house has been since Grandpa went on to heaven.

"Li'l sister, I been bringing Pa a hat for thirty years. I just couldn't come down South without a hat."

They put the new hat in Grandpa's casket, right beside his glasses. I will never understand a Jones funeral. You don't need your glasses in no casket because dead folks can't see. You sho' don't need no hat, like it's going to rain.

But it is fine with me that Aunt Rosie brought that hat. I just wish she would have left that crazy Collie up North. She come down here every summer with Aunt Rosie, Cousin Irene, and her mama, Aunt Louise, she cries from the time she get off the train to the time she leaves Rehobeth Road. Cries because she says she don't like "no South." Ma says if Miss Collie so citified, why is she saying "no South"? She is real light skinned, like her daddy's folks. So when she cries, she is red for a whole week. Grandma says there ain't no way in hell she listening to that mess for a week, so that foolish girl sits in the living room most of the time or she sleep. Sleep in my room.

I act just like she ain't here. She ain't no better than me and Chick-A-Boo. And if she think she is, she should see them bugs in the outhouse the next time she go in there to pee. They will bite her little red legs just like they bite ours. Ooh, that's it. She crying because she don't want to pee in the outhouse. Why didn't I figure out that Miss Collie did not want to pee outside five years ago? Well, I will have to fix that. In the morning I'm going to put some red ants in the outhouse for the city girl! Let's see how she likes that while she peeing!

"Grandma, are you going to give all of Grandpa's stuff to Mr. Charlie?"

"Hush up, Pattie Mae," Ma says.

"Let the child talk, Mer. She hurt just like you and me."

I can't believe my ears. Grandma actually thinks I can ask a question. Maybe this grown folks business will be over on Rehobeth Road sooner than later.

"Well, baby, we going to give away most of it," Grandma says real, real sad. "I thought I would save his hats for your uncle Buddy. Buddy can't wear his clothes because your grandpa was taller than him. I think I will give Buddy his hats and his shoeshine box."

My uncle Buddy always wanted that shoeshine box. Grandpa made it with his own two hands. He even made a footrest on each side of the box. I can't wait to find Uncle Buddy and tell him that the shoebox and all the polishes and rags are his now. He is going to look some kind of good in Grandpa's hats.

All night they separate clothes, even after they make me go to bed. I ain't putting up a fight, because I am so tired I don't know what to do. For a week we have been sitting up with folks who loved Grandpa. It seems that all of Rich Square has been by here to pay their respects. At least I know all of Rehobeth Road done been by here. From the time the colored undertaker Mr. Joe Gordon came and got Grandpa's body, folks have been piling in and out of Jones Property. When colored folks see that hearse leaving town, at least one person jump in their car and follow Mr. Gordon so they can find out who is dead. Then they take their nosy self right back to Rich

Square and tell the whole town. I don't know who followed Mr. Gordon up here when Grandpa died. I hear tell it was Flossie Boone's boy that they call Radio who followed Mr. Gordon to Jones Property. They call him Radio because he talks all the time. I do know that within one hour we had a house full of folks. That did not stop until tonight. My citified aunts are sick of our company and I am a little tired too, but the visitors are still our home people and that's the way we do stuff on Rehobeth Road. If my aunts don't like it they should take Collie and leave.

Me, I'm going to sleep right now.

In a few hours I'm right back out of bed. Grandpa's rooster crowing woke me up. That means it's morning. 5:30 in the morning. That is what time he crows. He thinks he is still waking up Grandpa. He don't know that Grandpa is dead. Dead and gone.

I don't think that roosters are as smart as cats and dogs, but I am going to go out there and tell that rooster to stop his crowing. I should yell,

"Shut up, old rooster! Grandpa can't hear you no more. Grandpa can't hear none of us!"

Well, maybe I shouldn't do that. Maybe I will just leave things the way they are. The rooster ain't bothering nobody but Collie. That fool screams every time the rooster crows. I laugh every time she screams.

I don't want too much to change around here. The rooster kind of makes you feel like things the same. He makes me remember how things use to be. How they were when Grandpa was alive. I want to look around and see Grandpa's face in the cotton, in the strawberry patch. I want to see his smile when I look down in the coffee that I ain't suppose to be drinking but Grandma gives to me anyway.

Yep, I think I will let that rooster keep on crowing and thinking that Grandpa is alive. It ain't hurting nobody.

Breakfast sure smells good. Ma cooking early like she do every day of her life. She cooking some extra eggs today because Bay Boy, who lives over in Scotland Neck, is here today to help Coy do some work around Jones Property. They have to move some beds to get to the rest of Grandpa's stuff. Bay Boy ain't no kin to us. He is about forty years old and he helped Grandpa and Uncle Buddy to build the other rooms onto this house. He has his own building company that he runs from the back of his truck. He just go from house to house helping folks to do whatever they need doing. Folks use to tell him he needed to get a job. They shut they mouth when he got that new truck and a new house all in one year. Grandpa told Bay Boy, "Now, Bay Boy, I ain't worked for the white man in forty years. You do not have to work for them either. You just keep on getting up in the morning, working hard, and mind your business. The Lord will pay your bills."

That's what Bay Boy did, and he and Grandpa have their own land. They own their own house and every piece of furniture in it. Grown folks can talk their heads off, but it ain't going to change nothing. And Bay Boy learned a lot from Grandpa.

I can hear Bay Boy in the kitchen just hollering

and carrying on like a woman. That's the reason he didn't come here after the funeral. Grandma told him to stay home, crying and carrying on. He know good and well he should not be in there crying and upsetting everybody all over again. But he miss Grandpa something bad. Now Ma crying and Aunt Louise done started that city hollering again. I peek in on crazy Collie and she done got back in my bed again and covered her head so she can't hear the hollering. She got a nerve, as much as she cry. My cousin Irene ain't paying them no attention, because she too busy packing. Packing because she said she done heard all the crying she can take. She said this is too much for her city nerves. Grandma walks in the kitchen and puts a stop to all this mess.

"Look a here, Bay Boy, Braxton Jones is dead. He is dead and he ain't coming back. I ain't never seen him cry in the whole fifty years that I was married to him, so I do not want to listen to you cry either. Now stop that mess."

Poor Bay Boy wipe his nose on his shirtsleeve and eat his breakfast. Ma runs out the back door to the barn to cry some more. Grandma don't care where she go as long as she leave her kitchen. She even grabbed the dishrag out of Ma's hand as she ran out of the door. Grandma ain't that softhearted about nothing.

She make herself a cup of coffee and start telling Bay Boy what to do. Coy was suppose to help, but she said, "Bay Boy can do this and you do the driving." Now she going to work Bay Boy to death. "Clean under the beds. Get them boxes out of the smokehouse. Go outside and get some wood for the stove. When you finish that, pick the weeds out of the flowers." The list just go on and on. She does not shut her mouth until Bay Boy starts telling her what he just heard about Uncle Buddy.

"Miss Babe, I got word about Buddy."

"Word from who?" She sounds real mad. "And why folks telling you, not me?"

"Well now, Miss Babe, ain't no reason to get mad. A few black Masons told me that Buddy definitely made it to Harlem and he just fine. They did not tell you because the law pass here all the time looking for Buddy. They know if a Mason come up here too much, then they just coming with news about Buddy. You know and I know that a Mason will end up in jail or dead. The law don't think much about me coming around because they know I use to help Mr. Braxton from time to time."

Grandma listen for a minute and then she start fussing again. "First of all, don't be telling me not to get mad, boy. I helped birth you into this world with your ma crying like she was having a cow. Second, if you had this news, why you just now telling me?"

Grandma should be shame of herself for talking to Bay Boy about his ma crying like a cow. She don't care nothing about hurting your feelings. Just because she delivered every colored baby in the county, she think she they mama. I don't care if she is my grandma, it ain't right. It just ain't right. Poor Bay Boy just can't win for losing. I just think I will go out back to Grandpa's old shed so that I will not have to listen to her telling the poor man off. Lord, she is getting louder!

Out in the shed, Ma louder than Grandma.

Jones Property is just loud this morning.

I can't see no peace nowhere so I might as well go back in the kitchen to save Bay Boy.

"Good morning, Grandma," I say. "Good morning, everybody." That's the way you speak when other people are in the house. You have to use Grandma's name first, then you can say "everybody" to the other folks. But you better say "Grandma" first. Let me tell you why. You have to live on Rehobeth Road to know what it is like to live around Babe Jones. She got her own rules and we follow them. She says to speak to her first because she is the oldest person on Rehobeth Road. She wasn't but two weeks older than Grandpa was. You think she care about that, but she don't. She care about having her way. Period!

We eat breakfast and wash the dishes in total silent. After breakfast we all pray one more time and start working around Jones Property. She's almost working us to death.

"Grandma, are we going to take the white sheet off the mirror in there where Collie is?"

"Yes, Pattie Mae, you can take the sheet off the mirror in Collie's room," Grandma says. "And you do not have to laugh at her to do it."

I'm just going to run into my bedroom where that crazy Miss Collie is and grab the sheet right off the mirror and scare her behind. Wrong again. I grabbed the sheet off the mirror and Miss Citified Collie just laughed at me. Good! Laugh your tail right out that door. Laugh all the way to the train station. Laugh all the way back to Harlem.

For the rest of the week, we work around Jones Property. Me, Hobo, and Hudson walk back and forth between Grandma's and the old slave house to get my clothes ready for my trip.

Chick-A-Boo said she is coming by to help me pack today.

"Hey, Chick-A-Boo."

"Hey, Pattie Mae," she says as I jump off of Grandpa's front porch to hug her. We always hug real tight. Chick-A-Boo said we should do this in case something happens to us, like what happen to June Bug and Willie.

Hobo barks at Chick-A-Boo like he always do.

He don't want her to touch me. Hudson could care less. They're all following me to the slave house. I think Hudson and Hobo are friends now that Grandpa is dead. They did not like each other much before that. I think Hudson didn't wanted to share Grandpa. Now they just got each other.

Me and Chick-A-Boo helping Ma wash at the slave house. It takes us half the day to finish washing all the dirty clothes. When we finish, we put all the clothes for my trip in a pillowcase and take them to Jones Property. Grandma said Ma do not iron worth a cuss. She is going to iron all the clothes I'm taking to Harlem.

Tomorrow we are leaving.

4

Headed North

*A*ll aboard!

The time has come and I am going North. North for the first time in my life.

Ma is staying here with her citified sisters and her crying niece. Cousin Irene left yesterday. Coy is staying too. He is going to do the driving for the women folks. Lord, do I feel sorry for him. Chick-A-Boo could have come to the train station, but she such a crybaby that she stayed on Rehobeth Road. Me, Hobo, and Hudson had to go tell her good-bye yesterday. I'm almost waving my hand off at Ma, Grandma, and Coy as we pulling off in the big train.

Just like I thought, BarJean done fell asleep after getting us a soda pop. When she wakes up I am going to tell her about the old one-tooth lady sitting across from us that asked me about Uncle Buddy. She is from Florida and she read all about him in the newspaper down there. The old lady is asleep now too.

Now that they both are sleep, I can go through some of these dead folks' obituaries. When I find Uncle Buddy, I am going to tell him that I finally got old enough to see the dead folks' papers. These papers are some kind of old, like Grandma Nicey's papers. But I can still read them. This one is for Miss Bessie Rou. Uncle Buddy was real good friends with her boy Massey. She use to live on Rehobeth Road with her husband, Mr. George. Mr. George is still on this earth, but Miss Bessie Rou is dead now and so are most of her children. Ma said she ain't never seen nothing to beat it. They all just started dying at one time.

When I open Miss Bessie Rou's dead folks' paper, it has all her children's papers folded inside. Her boy Perry, who use to be Coy's best friend, died first. I remember when word came to Rehobeth Road that he was in the hospital. Perry left home when he was sixteen, just like Coy. One day something that nobody knows but God happened on his job at a factory up in Harlem and he somehow got burned from his chest down. Burned real, real bad. He lived for about two weeks and then he went on to meet his maker. The call came to Mr. Bay's that poor Perry was dead. One of Perry's cousins called Mr. Bay because he was the only person on Rehobeth Road with a phone. It was early one Saturday morning when Mr. Bay walked to the path of Jones Property and yelled to Grandpa. I was playing in the front yard when he came over there.

"Braxton Jones, you home?"

"Grandpa, Mr. Bay calling for you," I yelled into the house.

Grandpa came out on the porch and yelled back. "I'm right here. Bay, what in the world is wrong?"

"That boy of George's, Perry, is dead. You best tell them."

Then he turned around and went back to Bay's Property. That was a mean way to tell us about poor Perry. Grandpa got his cane and walked off of Jones Property and did not say a word. Me, Hobo, and Hudson followed him. Grandma had heard Mr. Bay and Grandpa talking, so she covered the mirrors and changed into her black dress. Then she got her cane and walked over to Miss Doleebuck's house so that they could go down to see about Miss Bessie Rou. She was washing some white sheets on the back porch when Grandpa and me got there.

"Bessie Rou, how you this morning?"

"I'm making it, Braxton Jones. What you doing up here so . . ." She stopped in the middle of her sentence and looked Grandpa in the face real hard. "No, Braxton, don't you come up here with death. Please don't come with death. Get off this land with death."

Then she threw the wet sheets on the ground and fell down on the porch with a loud thump. Lord, that woman did some crying. I cried too. Hobo howled because he knew death was here.

Hudson ran like he did when Grandpa died last week. He ran away from death. Mr. George came out on the porch and sat down behind his wife body that was like a dishrag by then. I just rubbed poor Miss Bessie Rou's head until Grandma and Miss Doleebuck got there. When they got there, they saw a sad sight. Miss Bessie Rou was still lying on the back porch crying. The women folks took over and I was glad. That was a sad day on Rehobeth Road and little did we know the worse was coming for Miss Bessie Rou and Mr. George. The funeral was so sad and when it was over, we never mentioned Perry's name around Miss Bessie Rou again because she would throw a fit. Her children took it hard too, and her oldest boy, Massey, who had come down from Harlem for Perry's funeral, said he was not going back. He said his folks was too broken up to live by themselves, so he stayed. Matter of a fact, he never made it back to Harlem at all. Not ever!

Trying to cheer Miss Bessie Rou up, the children on Rehobeth Road started to play stickball in her front yard on Saturdays, instead of in the field right beside Mr. Charlie's house. Coy was home from Harlem, so we were having a good time. It was a Saturday and Mr. Massey was doing what he did every Saturday that God sent since he moved back to Rehobeth Road. He washed his black Chevy and polished it until we could see our faces reflecting on the door. I was on first base. Chick-A-Boo was on second base. Chick-A-Boo's brother, Randy, was on third. Coy was at bat. He hit the ball. A home run. "Run, Pattie Mae, run!" Massey yelled as he shined and shined his car. We all made it home. Four home runs. A grand slam!

"I did it, Mr. Massey. I did it." I looked over to Mr. Massey and his face had a look of horror on it. Lord, did the ball hit Mr. Massey?

No! It was death.

He fell to the ground as his face turned as green as the grass. We ran to him.

"Mr. Massey! Mr. Massey!" we screamed.

"Get back! Get back!" Coy yelled. Miss Bessie Rou was sitting on the front porch making a quilt out of all of Perry's clothes that her children had brought from Harlem.

"Massey, Massey," she cried out as she ran to the car, dropping the quilt. "Lord, no, Lord, no, not another child of mine."

Mr. Massey was as dead as Perry. Folks say he had a heart attack. I just started running like I had never run before. Hudson was running beside me and Hobo, until he ran straight under the house at Grandpa's. He was running from death. I ran right past Jones Property up to the slave house where I knew Ma was making biscuits for Saturday supper. I don't know why I passed Jones Property. I just did.

"Ma, Ma, come quick. Mr. Massey done fell dead."

Ma threw the dough down on the table and wiped her hands right on her dress. Ma can run. She ran right past Jones Property too.

"Pattie Mae," Ma said in between breaths, "get Pa and Ma Babe."

I turned onto Jones Property and Ma kept on going. I don't remember turning. I don't remember opening the back door. Grandpa was in the kitchen getting ready to take some leftover food out to Hudson and Hobo.

"Child, what in the sand hill is wrong?" Grandpa asked.

"Grandpa, come with me! Mr. Massey done fell dead in Miss Bessie Rou's yard!"

He grabbed his cane and started walking back down death road one more time. I walk with him. Me and Hobo. He stopped and got Mr. Charlie. Miss Doleebuck waited on the front porch for Grandma, who was covering the mirrors and putting on her black dress.

By now Randy had ran up to Mr. Bay's with a quarter to use the phone. That Mr. Bay should be shamed of himself for charging us a quarter to make a phone call. Not anymore, though, because Grandma got a phone now. A yellow phone.

It did not take long for Mr. Joe Gordon to get there. Before he got there, Ma took poor Miss Bessie Rou's half-made quilt and covered Mr. Massey up in it. They had to drag Miss Bessie Rou in the house.

"Massey and Perry, Massey and Perry," she cried out for her boys the rest of the day.

Another death on Rehobeth Road. Another

funeral. The funeral was at Chapel Hill that next Saturday. When the preacher started to preach, he said some good things about Mr. Massey, but right in the middle of his preaching he said, "Bessie Rou, we know you hurt. We know what it's like to lose two sons in two months."

That was the wrong thing to say to her.

In her grief Miss Bessie Rou had lost her mind.

"You don't know a damn thang!" she yelled back.

The church fell silent. Randy got tickled and laughed out loud. Tickled ain't all he got. According to Chick-A-Boo, Randy got the whipping of his life when he got home.

It took a long time for things to get back to normal on Rehobeth Road. It took a long time for folks to forget that Miss Bessie Rou yelled at the preacher man. Many funerals would follow for that family. I just stopped going after a while. Within two years Miss Bessie Rou's girl Roe Mae fell dead in the grocery store. Her boy Wesley James died up in Harlem. And Miss Bessie Rou herself died of who knows what. I reckon her heart just broke in half.

Mr. George, he still alive down there on Cumbo Road, where he moved in with his girl Hattie James, who was Wesley James's twin. When it was all said and done, I think more folks died in that family in two years than all of the folks that died on Rehobeth Road in my whole life.

I keep thinking about all those people as this train moves north taking me to a place I ain't never been before. I hope I will like Harlem. It can't be as lonely as it gets on Rehobeth Road, mainly when the milkman don't blow. I think I'll tell Uncle Buddy what the milkman done to me. Abusing a twelve-year-old. Uncle Buddy will go right over there and tell him a piece of his mind. BarJean and the old lady still sleep and I am going to read until one of them wake up. I don't know the old lady, but I know she will ask even more questions if she see my obituaries.

5

June Bug

This obituary is for June Bug and his cousin Willie. I remember when they died. Willie lived back in the Low Meadows. Willie wasn't no kin to me, but June Bug's ma is my Aunt Rosie. They were visiting from Harlem for Christmas when he meet his maker. My Big Aunt Sally, who was Grandpa's sister, was keeping them back in the Low Meadows so that they would help her pack pecans for Christmas presents. The Low Meadows is a place off of Bryantown Road with a long dirt path. The land was already low and after the big rain came in 1940, Ma said there was a flood and it washed away two inches of land. The only reason Big Aunt Sally house is still standing is because it was up on the hillside. It's empty now, because she died two months after the boys died.

Anyway, we called her Big Aunt Sally because Ma had a baby sister named Sally, who the family had planned to call Little Aunt Sally, but she died. Ma said that her sister Sally was sleeping with Grandma and Grandpa when one of them rolled over and suffocated her to death in the middle of the night. They don't know who rolled over on her. They just know she was dead the next morning.

Big Aunt Sally was real nice. I helped her, June Bug, and Willie pack pecans for a week until Ma made me come home. I am so glad I was not there when them boys died that I do not know what to do.

Big Aunt Sally been telling us all our lives not to go back of the field to the pond. Well, June Bug and Willie was hardheaded and went back there anyway. They had been back there twice before the day death came. Both times I told Big Aunt Sally and she took a switch to they behinds. That did not do any good. Big Aunt Sally was sweeping the front porch when Willie and June Bug came running around the house talking about they going for a walk.

"You both can walk all you want to, but you best not go near that pond."

"We won't, Big Aunt Sally."

Willie's ma, Essie, was out Christmas shopping at the thrift store over in Jackson when all of this happen. I don't know why them boys did not listen, because they dead for not listening.

The day my cousin and Willie died there was another boy at the pond that we call Hog Daddy. We call him Hog Daddy because he eat like a hog and he looks just like his daddy. He eats all the time just like Toe Worm. From house to house, he go telling lies to grown folks. He tells them that he hungry because he ain't ate nothing. They feed him, then he go to another house and tell another grown-up the same lie until his belly is full. Hog Daddy had stopped by Big Aunt Sally's for blackberry dumplings the day the boys died. He claims he could not skate because he had a belly full from eating Big Aunt Sally's blackberry dumplings. He lying! Who goes to a pond in December unless they going to ice-skate?

The sun had been shining all day and that ice was mighty thin. Hog Daddy said that Willie got on the ice first and skated all the way to the middle. Hog Daddy said before he could say "no," Willie fell through the ice, yelling at the top of his lungs. June Bug yelled and skated out there too. Skated out there to save Willie. Down he went! Them boys couldn't even swim. Hog Daddy ain't no kin to them, but he almost died trying to save their lives. He said he pulled them out one by one. Willie was dead and Hog Daddy knew it, but June Bug was still breathing, so Hog Daddy laid Willie by the side of the pond and carried June Bug all the way back to Big Aunt Sally's house on his back. It was too late, June Bug died right there on Big Aunt Sally's living-room floor. Then Big Aunt Sally had to walk all the way out of the Low Meadows to tell Aunt Rosie that her boy was dead. Hog

Daddy had to walk to town to get Joe Gordon, because Big Aunt Sally did not have a telephone.

Aunt Rosie was at church decorating for the Christmas party. Ma said she hollered for five hours. Grandpa said he could hear her on Rehobeth Road. That's five miles from the church where Aunt Rosie was doing her hollering.

That's the truth.

Two caskets, not one.

Two families, not one.

Two hearses, not one.

I can't think about it another minute. I want to think about finding Uncle Buddy. When I do, we are going to talk about the living, not the dead.

6

Harlem, Lord, Harlem

I wonder how big Harlem is. For sure it is bigger than Rehobeth Road. For sure it is bigger than Rich Square. I hope it ain't too hard to find my uncle.

Before Grandpa died, I overheard him tell Grandma that Uncle Buddy is right here in Harlem. Well, I didn't overhear him tell her nothing. I was ease dropping. Yes, I know it's rude, but that's the only way to get my information from grown folks. I just take my mason jar and put it to the door and get me an ear full. I sure hope they got mason jars up North. I have got to get me a mason jar. If I can't find one, I am going to send Chick-A-Boo a few quarters and she can mail me one. I miss Chick-A-Boo already. Before I left she told me she did not want to be called Chick-A-Boo after she turns thirteen next December. She wants to be called by her real name, Caroline. She done lost her mind. The first thing I am going to say when I see her little face is, "Chick-A-Boo, Chick-A-Boo, Chick-A-Booooooooooooooooooooo!"

I'm thinking about Chick-A-Boo and folks back home as the train is rolling into New York's Penn Station. BarJean said from here we are taking a taxicab to her apartment. I ain't never been in a taxicab before. I wonder if it is as big as Mr. Charlie's car. I'm so excited as we get in the taxicab.

All I can see is lights, lights, and more lights. I just believe I am going to faint. It's a sight for my eyes to see. People everywhere like it ain't even nighttime. I'm trying to see everything. Trying to count every light, but there are just too many. It is quite a ways to BarJean's apartment from the train station because we still riding. It's at least fifteen miles. I got butterflies from all this excitement. BarJean looking at me like she think I have lost my mind. But I ain't crazy; I'm just free. Free from chopping them fields on Rehobeth Road. Free from picking cotton come fall. Lord, I'm free from picking strawberries with Grandma until I can hardly stand up.

Grandma, I hope that she is feeling better. In silence she sure did take Grandpa's dying kinda hard. But I know Mr. Charlie and Miss Doleebuck will check on Grandma every day. And Ma ain't going to never stop going to Jones Property.

I wonder what Mr. Charlie going to do for a best friend now that Grandpa done met his maker. He'll probably do nothing because Grandpa said you only have one best friend in a lifetime. Best friends like me and Chick-A-Boo. We were born and raised right there on Rehobeth Road together, and she will always be my best friend. On second thought, I love Chick-A-Boo so much that I will think about calling her Caroline for one week when I get back to Rehobeth Road. Lord, we all been through some stuff this summer and where in the world is my uncle Buddy? I can tell you one thing, if he is here in Harlem, I am going to find him. Yes sir, sure as the sunrise in the morning, I am going to start looking for Uncle Buddy. There ain't a building in Harlem big enough to hide Uncle Buddy from me.

Look at this place. We passing the Apollo Theater now. Just look at all the lights. The sign says DUKE ELLINGTON in big lights out front. I wish I could go inside. I wish I could see Mr. Ellington in person. Miss Nora got a picture of him in her pocketbook. She told me that she and Uncle Buddy go to the Savoy Club on Lenox Avenue and dance to his music all night. That's a nightclub for colored folks, according to Miss Nora.

When I told Miss Nora BarJean's address, she said it's not far from where the Cotton Club used to be, but BarJean lives closer to the Savoy. The Cotton Club is the place where Mr. Ellington played his music years ago, but colored folks couldn't go in. That's a shame that white folks like our music, but they do not like us. Now black folks can go in the Savoy. Lord, there it is! The Savoy! It's a line of folks wrapped around the building.

The taxicab driver finally pulls up in front of a big redbrick building.

"This is where I live, Pattie Mae," BarJean says as the taxicab driver stops along the sidewalk. I see in real life the redbrick two-story building that she had already showed me in the pictures on the same day she came home for Grandpa's funeral.

I can't move! I can't move one inch!

A real apartment building that I am going to spend the night in. Not just one night, but a few weeks. I can't believe it.

"That will be two dollars, miss," the driver says to BarJean. She reach in her faded brown bag to pay him. See there, Grandma cannot come to Harlem. Right here in the middle of the street she would be putting her hand in her bra to take out her money.

I can't believe that driver ain't helping us get our bags out of the boot of the car. As soon as he drives off, I'm going to speak about how this man is acting.

Off he goes with his no-manners self.

"That man didn't even help us take our clothes out of the boot," I say to BarJean. Suddenly I believe BarJean is going to have a fit. But she ain't even mad about the rude taxicab driver. She mad at *me*.

"Boot! Pattie Mae, don't say the word *boot* here in Harlem. Say *trunk*. The trunk of the car."

Harlem sure does change folks. BarJean know good and well we don't say the word trunk on Rehobeth Road, we say boot. She ought to be shame of herself. She really should. When I see Uncle Buddy, I am going to tell him about how citified she trying to be. All the way to the third floor, while we climbing the stairs I am thinking about Miss BarJean's mess.

So this is what an apartment looks like. Just like on TV. I just know heaven ain't no better than this. It ain't. It can't be. I'm going to sit my suitcase down and go straight to the bathroom. A real toilet! Not an outhouse. A sink, not a face tub. I can feel BarJean breathing down my neck just because I am still standing in this door looking at her bathroom. She might as well go somewhere and sit her fast self down, because I'm going to look at this bathroom until I get sleepy.

Maybe she does call the boot a trunk now, but she knows a bathroom ain't no outhouse. She knows what it feels like to want to get up in the middle of the night to pee but you hold it till mornin' cause the fire done gone out in the woodstove and it's just too cold to get out of bed. Them nights when you can't hold it no more, your pee freeze before it hit the bottom of the pee pot. She knows what that's like. She knows what it's like to go in the kitchen to warm your bath water and it's cold before you get it back to the bedroom to take a bath. If Miss Citified don't remember nothing else, she remember them snakes running her out of the outhouse before she can pee. And I bet you a million dollars that she use to pray for a bathroom before she got her monthly period, just like I do now.

"So, how do you like it?" she asks, while I'm rubbing the sink like I am waiting for it to come alive.

"I like it, sister, I like it just fine."

"Well, good. You can take a bath in the morning."

"In the morning? Can I take a bubble bath now?"

"You can, city girl," BarJean say with a laugh.

She reach to the back of the tub and gives me some bubble bath. I really am going to die. I ain't never used real bubble bath before. When I take a bath in the big tub on Rehobeth Road, I just use a little lye soap that Ma makes three times a year. She makes that lye soap to sale to Mr. Wilson at the grocery store. I'm going to take Ma some of this bubble bath.

I just have to turn the faucet on and watch the bubbles and water fill the tub to the top. As my behind touch the bottom of the tub I can feel a tear rolling down my face.

Maybe I am going to be a city girl after all. Me and Uncle Buddy use to talk about it for hours. I can hear him now.

"Now, Pattie Mae, be careful not to let the cotton bows stick in your hands. City girls got nice hands."

I have to close my eyes tight. Real tight, so I can just see Uncle Buddy's face. See his smile. I miss him. But I know he's safe. He's alive. Not dead, like them people in the obituaries.

I'm not going to think about dead folks right now, because I might get to hollering right here in this tub. Instead, I stay in the tub until the water gets cold.

BarJean fitted me a nice bed. Those sheets ain't white like Ma's and Grandma's. They pink and they smell so, so good.

I peek out the window and just like Miss Nora said, it's beauty here in Harlem. Black folks walking down the streets all dressed up. I don't know how I'm going to sleep tonight. It seems like morning ain't never going to come. I just want the sun to shine. I want the rooster to crow. Lord, what am I saying? Ain't no rooster going to crow in the morning. I'm in Harlem now. Ain't no rooster here in the city at all.

. . .

I don't need nobody to tell me it's morning now because I can hear BarJean moving around in the kitchen. She got to be back at work today because she done missed a whole week's work when she was down South with us for the funeral. She singing away just like Ma. I can hear her real good, because my little room is right next to the kitchen just like it is at our house down home. She don't sound as good as Ma. Ma can sing, "May the Work I've Done" all she want to. And I tell you another thing, Ma can praise God and sing at the same time. Yep, she sing stuff like "May the work I've done speak for me." Right in the middle of a note, she will scream "Yes, Lord, yesssssssssssss!" BarJean don't know how to do that yet. I don't even have to get out of bed to talk to my big sister. I can just yell across the room.

"Good morning," I say, trying to sound like a city girl.

"Good morning, sleeping beauty. How did you sleep last night?"

"I didn't sleep much. Just excited, I guess."

"You can get some sleep today. I have to work until five and it takes me about thirty minutes to walk home. You know the rules. No going outside, and call downstairs to Miss Sylvine place if there is any trouble. Her telephone number is right here on the icebox. Most of all, do not open that door for nobody but Miss Sylvine, Coy, and me."

I don't know what she talking about Coy for; he ain't even back from down South yet. I know them women folks are about to drive him crazy. Crazy as a bedbug. When he get back to Harlem, he will have to sleep for a week.

"But I don't know what Miss Sylvine looks like," I say, hoping for a brief telling of the woman.

"You don't need to know what she looks like. She is from down home just like us. Her voice tells who she is."

BarJean right about folks on Rehobeth Road. They all talk just alike: Country! Country! Country!

"Besides she has never seen you, missy. So there! You don't know each other. I will take you

66

downstairs when I get home so you two can meet."

I know not to ask another question. As a matter of a fact, I will just shut up, period. BarJean just like Ma. She done made up her mind what I'm suppose to say and do. That's that.

I got to get up, walk in this kitchen, and watch BarJean finish cooking breakfast. She can't fry an egg, so this is going to be some meal.

She really looks like Ma. She fuss just like her too. She can fuss all she wants to. The minute she walks out that front door I'm leaving this apartment so I can find my uncle. You know, I bet he done found himself a new city woman and forgot all about Miss Nora. If that's what he has done, he ought to be shame of himself. I'm not going to mention that to BarJean, because if I do she is just going to tell me that's grown folks business, and she will force me to use the mason jar here, too.

When BarJean turns the water on to make her a cup of coffee, I almost jump out of my skin. The only time I have ever heard the sound of running water before in my whole life is at the schoolhouse and when I took my bubble bath last night.

"What's wrong with you, girl?" BarJean says while she is laughing at me.

"Nothing, I just ain't use to no running water in the house."

"Ain't it something, little sister, how we did without so much all our lives?" she says in between a laugh and almost crying.

She didn't say nothing after that. We just sitting here looking at each other. Looking at each other like we know something that other folks don't know. Things that only folks that were born and raised on Rehobeth Road know. Rehobeth Road is a strange place. The houses are old and the white folks are long gone. All except Mr. Bay, who is getting on up there in years.

The colored folks that live on Rehobeth Road don't own nothing but the shirts on their backs. Everybody except Grandpa. He owned Jones Property, and now that he done met his maker, my grandma owns Jones Property. When she leaves this earth, it will belong to my ma and her sisters.

When they leave here, Jones Property will belong to the grandchildren. That's the way Grandpa wanted it and that's the way it is. He said Jones Property ain't never to be sold. Never!

"All right, Miss Pattie Mae, I'm leaving for work now."

"Oh, sister, don't worry. All I am going to do today is sleep. I promise you that." I have my legs crossed under the table because I'm trying to break the lie. Chick-A-Boo says if you tell a lie for a good reason you should cross your fingers or your legs and the Lord will forgive you. I am definitely lying because as soon as BarJean goes to work, I'm going out the door.

"Bye," BarJean yells as she is walking out the door.

Just wait till I find Uncle Buddy. I'm going to tell him about her talking about don't say the word *boot*. Well, maybe I will tell him that after I tell him that they caught them mean white folks who tried to hang him. Wait till I tell him that they are going to have a trial for them mean men. The day right before Grandpa's funeral, they caught the seven men who tried to kill Uncle Buddy. They all going to court for kidnapping in a few weeks. After I tell Uncle Buddy the mean men are going to court, I think he will want to come home. Back down South. Back to Rehobeth Road where he belongs. Somewhere in this grown folks conversation, I will have to tell him about Grandpa done met the man upstairs. Then I will show him the obituary. I'm going to tell him all about Hassie Lee reading it aloud at the funeral. Hassie Lee is the church secretary. She always reads the obituary.

Ma put poems and stuff the people in town and on Rehobeth Road told her to write in the obituary. In the space where Ma wrote who was singing the solos, she wrote my friend Daniel's mama, Miss Novella's, name twice because she did all the singing. Miss Blanche, Chick-A-Boo's ma, can sing too, but not like Miss Novella. Miss Novella sings, "May the Work I've Done" better than Ma can. Now, that was Grandpa's favorite song, probably because he done heard Ma sing it till her voice ran dry. Miss Novella got bad knees, but ain't nothing wrong with her mouth. When she opened her mouth at Grandpa's funeral, it sound like heaven was right here on earth. She rocks from side to side when she sings. At Grandpa's funeral she got to rocking and shouting, but she never stop singing. The other women in the choir took their obituaries and went to fanning Miss Novella. She sang louder when they cooled her off. She got children that can sing too. That Pearl can sing all she want to. She lives somewhere up here in Harlem and I heard that she was on the radio a few times. Miss Novella's baby girl Dorothy sings at school on Jamboree Night. Miss Clark, who moved to Rich Square from Carr, North Carolina, to teach us biology, started Jamboree Night. I don't know what they do in Carr, but Miss Clark said there was nothing to do in Rich Square so she started this talent show every Saturday night at Creecy School in the gym. Ain't no need to enter the talent show if Dorothy is in it because you can't outsing her and you sho' can't outdance her. She moves like she ain't got no bones in her body. Miss Novella said she better not be shaking her bottom parts. Honey, please! Everything on that Dorothy girl shakes. She got talent like her mama, who sang so loud at Grandpa's funeral that I know he heard her. Yes, he did.

7

The Walk

I'm all dressed now and all I have to do is get past Miss Sylvine's door downstairs without getting caught. I'm wearing my red short pants that Uncle Buddy gave me and a white blouse that was too big for Chick-A-Boo. She said I can wear it until she is big enough to wear her own blouse. Then she said I got to give it back to her. I might and I might not.

I am just about to open the door when I hear folk talking downstairs.

"Good morning."

"Good morning, Gloria."

"Where you off to so early in the morning, Miss Sylvine?"

"I'm going to a meeting over at the church."

Well, they just made my day. Miss Sylvine is leaving and this Gloria person ain't nobody that BarJean ever mentioned to me. So I'll just leave when they finish gossiping in the hallway.

Soon as Miss Sylvine leaves, I make my escape.

This street feels like it is paved with gold. I want to cry. You don't know what it is like to want to be in a place like this while you in a hot peanut field chopping weeds. Sometimes I think I just chopped up a half a row of peanuts daydreaming about Harlem. Now I am here. Thank you, God. Look at these people. They don't know what my little twelve-year-old heart has been through. Ohhhhh, they so dressed up. I am glad I got Chick-A-Boo's new blouse on. I don't know if I look like a city girl, but I feel like one.

Everyone in Harlem must have a job because ain't too many folks walking the streets this morning. The few that are walking around ain't even noticed me. Even if they do, they don't know me from Adam.

One thing for sure, folks here ain't as nosy as folks back home. Let me just try to walk down Main Street at home without Ma. Before my heels could hit the ground, someone would be on Rehobeth Road to tattle to Ma. If they can't find her, they going straight to Jones Property to tattle to Grandma.

Look at this place. Look at all these stores. There is even a grocery store on the bottom floor of BarJean's building. I better not go in there because I bet you the shoes I'm wearing BarJean has told everybody in there to keep an eye on me.

Uncle Buddy said all these people in Harlem are from down South, but they don't look like it. They look like they been up here all they lives. They come here so they can get some respect. Uncle Buddy said he didn't know what it felt like to be treated like a man until he came up here to Harlem. Maybe he should have stayed up here. Yep, maybe he should stay here now. Maybe it ain't right for me to want him to come back home with me. If Uncle Buddy had not come back to Rehobeth Road in 1942, he would have never got in the mess he in today. Till this day, we don't really know why he came back. He wrote us a letter one day and said he was coming home soon. Home! That very next Sunday morning, there he was. For five years he lived on Rehobeth Road in peace and worked at the sawmill in Rich Square. At least he did until that terrible Friday night. That would have never happened to him here in Harlem. Now I have to find him and tell him they caught the white men who tried to kill him. I have to tell him they going to give him a trial too. At his trial Uncle Buddy can tell them that he didn't try to hurt that white woman. He can't tell the truth if he don't want to go home.

It sure feels nice walking down this street with cars passing. Don't many cars come on Rehobeth Road, except for Mr. Charlie and folks that farming. White folks and Randy ride up and down Rehobeth Road all summer. Ole Man Taylor owns most of

Rehobeth Road and he let Randy, who ain't old enough to drive, do all of his driving. Of course you see the milkman. Other than that, you don't see a soul from sunrise to sunset. But here in Harlem, cars are everywhere. Right in front of my eyes. It's too many to count. But I better stop looking at these cars and pay attention to the street signs so that I will not get lost or worse. I might get hit by a car the way Flossie Mae's brother, Wink, did last year.

For the life of me, I can't figure out how you get hit by a car on Rehobeth Road. You can hear a car coming a mile away because it's so quiet around there. Mr. Bud was driving over to see Grandpa when Wink stepped out in front of his car and it knocked him clean into Mr. Bay's cow pasture. He better be glad he wasn't hurt too bad to run, because them bulls had started coming toward him. Old as Mr. Bud is, he jumped that fence and helped Wink out with a broken arm before the bulls broke all his bones. If that boy had not got out, his obituary would be in that chest on Jones Property too. Right beside the paper for Mr. Bud, who died last winter.

First stop, a candy store.

Everybody in here look like they know I'm from Rehobeth Road. They looking at me funny. Maybe they know Uncle Buddy. As soon as I pay for my candy, I'm going to ask the storekeeper about my uncle.

"Can I help you, young lady?" the storekeeper asks when he see me looking in the glass case that is filled with candy and bubble gum.

"Yes, sir, I would like two chocolate drops."

"Two chocolate drops it is. What a nice little voice. And just where are you from?"

"North Carolina, sir."

"Don't know why I asked. Your Southern drawl is a dead giveaway."

Oh, Lord, these city folks are a mess. He sounds like he from back of Grandpa's field and he talking about *my* accent.

"Where you from, sir?"

"South Carolina."

He got some nerves. I saw South Carolina on a map at school and accordingly to that map South Carolina is farther south than North Carolina. But

I will just let him think he sounds citified.

"Do you know a man named Goodwin Bush?" I ask.

He stop dead in his tracks.

"What you doing asking about Buddy, child?"

He knows my uncle.

"Well, I read about him in the paper and I just wanted to know if you know him."

"Everyone in Harlem know Buddy. And we know what them white folks down home tried to do to him. So don't you go asking a bunch of folks around here about Buddy unless you want to get yourself in a world of trouble. White folks looking for him and I don't want no problems in my store."

"But I ain't white, sir."

"Don't make no difference. We don't talk about Buddy here in Harlem. And don't you back talk me. Now run along."

"Yes, sir." I pay for my candy and get out of his store.

This is going to be harder than I thought. But one thing I know for sure now. Uncle Buddy is here in Harlem. If he was not here, why would that man act like that? They are hiding Uncle Buddy from the law.

Maybe if I walk a little farther, I will ask someone else. Maybe I will run into someone with a big mouth and they will tell me everything I need to know. I'm not getting very far because I have to stop and look in every store window. It is something to see, all right. One store has clothes hanging in the window on big dolls. The prettiest dresses I have ever seen. Well, maybe not as pretty as the dresses that Grandma makes. Her dresses got love in them.

My Lord, I believe a colored person own this dress store. 'Cause ain't nothing in there but colored folks.

Reckon it's true that colored folks really own Harlem. I love it here already. A colored woman inside the store who just walked up to the window, she's smiling at me. I smile back and wave. She looking like she ain't got much time for children, so I better not ask her about Uncle Buddy. I think I'll just go in and look at all the pretty clothes.

I walk inside and before I know it, the woman standing over me. She smells like grandma's rose garden.

"Good morning, young lady. Can I help you?"

"No, ma'am, I'm just looking at the pretty dresses."

"That's just fine, but what are you doing walking the streets alone?"

"Well, my sister is at work and I thought I would take a walk."

"Taking a walk? You must be from the South."

"Yes, ma'am, I am. But how did you know that?"

"Because, honey, up here folks don't let their children walk the streets alone day or night."

"But why not?"

"Why not? Child, this ain't down home. This is the big city. Now you go on home and wait for your sister to get off work."

Everyone here is just as bossy as the people down home. I go back on the street.

That lady ain't my ma and she don't know my ma, so I ain't going home just cause she say so. I'm just going to walk until I get tired. Uncle Buddy probably ain't found no job that quick, so he might be out here walking the streets too. He could have on a hat and glasses so that people will not know who he is. But I will know him no matter what he is wearing.

Every store looks different. Filled with everything from candles to plants and furniture. One store here has more stuff than all the stores in Rich Square got put together.

I'm getting hungry. My chocolate drops wore off so maybe I better head home for something to eat. Then I'll go out again later to keep on looking for Uncle Buddy.

It don't take me long to get back to the apartment. I use the key that BarJean gave me this morning and go through the front door of the building as I pray Miss Sylvine don't see me. Lord, I'm glad to be back inside. It's almost as hot walking the streets of Harlem as it is working in the fields. Well, not quite.

I think I will just make myself a peanut butter and jelly sandwich. BarJean sure do keep a lot of food in her pantry. She probably don't want me to say pantry. Let's see. What word can I use for pantry? Maybe closet will do. I will ask Miss City BarJean when she gets home. Right now I just want to sleep for a minute before lunch.

I was going to go back out to look for Uncle Buddy again, but when I woke up, BarJean was putting her key in the front door. I guess I was tired after all. I'll start again tomorrow.

8

South of Baltimore

*F*or a whole week I get up every day and do the same thing. Walk and look, look and walk. BarJean does the same thing every day too. She gets up and has her coffee, get dressed, and she is out the door to work at the factory. She said when Saturday comes she is going to take me to buy some fabric to make my new school clothes. And she said she is going to get my hair pressed and maybe even let me get my ears pierced. Ma ain't going to like that. Ma ain't never had her ears pierced. She said if God wanted us to have a second hole in our ears for earrings he would have put two there, not one! I will worry about Ma when I get back home. While I'm here I'm going to do everything I can to look like a city girl. Ain't no need to come all the way up here and go home looking like you still a field hand.

And while I'm getting citified I will keep looking for my uncle.

But he ain't nowhere to be found. Nowhere!

"Good morning, little lady," a man in a white shirt says as I walk past his shoeshine stand.

"Good morning, sir."

He smiles and keeps on shining the black shoes of a man who is dressed like he on his way to church. He is writing away on a piece of yellow paper.

"What are you writing, sir?" I ask without thinking first.

"A novel."

"You mean like Mark Twain's *Tom Sawyer?*"

"No, like Richard Wright."

"Richard Wright. Well, I never heard of him."

"Little girl, you should know who Richard

Wright is if you know who Mark Twain is," the shoeshine man says.

"But everyone read Mark Twain's book."

"That's real good and they should. But every little black girl in Harlem reads Richard Wright's books."

"Who is Richard Wright?"

Now I know I said something stupid. The shoeshine man stop shining and the man in his chair stop smiling and look at me. He said:

"*I* am Richard Wright."

"You mean, you are a real writer? Why, sir, I didn't know there were colored writers!"

"Well, there are black writers and you should know all about them."

"Them. You mean there's more than one?"

"Why, sure. There's Langston Hughes, who lives right across the street. There's Zora Hurston, who lives a few blocks away, and Dorothy West, too."

"Women! Colored women writers?" I can't believe what I am hearing.

"Yes, child. And you should know who the black writers are."

He is saying black, not colored. I'm not going to ever say colored again.

"Well, I don't know who the black writers are. Do you know who Buddy Bush is?"

The shoeshine man stand up fast. "Girl, who are you and where did you come from?" he says.

"Sir, I'm from down South and I'm looking for Buddy Bush."

Mr. Wright don't seem to know or care who we are talking about, but this shoeshine man definitely knows my uncle. He grabs my arm and pulls me around the side of the building.

"Child, don't you know better than to come around here asking about Buddy?"

"But I have to find him."

"Find him for what? Don't you know the law is looking for him?"

"Yes, sir, that's the reason I have to find him. I have to tell him that they caught the men who tried to hang him. I have to tell him that it's okay to come home."

"Home! Child, what are you talking about? Harlem is Buddy's home now. He can't ever go down South again!"

"But he has to. Grandma wants him to come home."

"Grandma? You mean Miss Babe Jones?" Then he looks at me real hard. "Good God from Zion, you must be Pattie Mae Sheals!"

The shoeshine man done forgot all about Mr. Wright. How on earth does this man know my name? He is hugging me so tight I can't breathe.

"Don't be afraid, child. I'm Tom. I'm Mr. Charlie and Miss Doleebuck boy."

I just look at him. "But I know all of Mr. Charlie's children," I say. Then I remember the missing boy that ain't been south of Baltimore since he left all them years ago.

"All but me. I don't go down South for nothing. And I told Buddy to stay away from down there, but he would not listen. A colored man ain't got no business south of Baltimore. None!"

He looks sad as Mr. Wright comes around the corner to pay him two quarters.

"I'll see you next week, Tom, before I go back to Paris."

Paris! I almost fall on the ground. He lives in Paris, France. He just visiting New York. I'm going to ask Mr. Tom about that as soon as I find out where Uncle Buddy is.

"Yes sir, Mr. Wright. I will see you next time." Mr. Tom thanks Mr. Wright and turns back to me. "Pattie Mae, go on home."

"No, I can't go home. Not until you tell me where my uncle is."

"Look! Go home. Come back tomorrow at the same time. Now, go!"

I better do as I am told. If Mr. Tom knows Grandma got a telephone, he might call down there and tell her that I am up here looking for Uncle Buddy. If that happens Ma is going to skin me alive.

I am halfway home when I remember that I did not ask Mr. Tom about Mr. Wright living in Paris. I will have to ask him tomorrow.

Tonight I don't say a word to BarJean about running into Mr. Tom. We are eating catfish just like we do every Friday down South and then we are going to bed. I will read some more obituaries until I fall asleep. BarJean works a half day on Saturday so I will be back at the shoeshine stand at ten o'clock in the morning.

9

The Gravediggers

"Good morning, Mr. Tom."

"Good morning, child. How you feeling this morning?"

"I'm fine. Did you find my uncle?"

"Pattie Mae Sheals, what are you doing here, gal?"

I feel love come all over my body. A love that only Uncle Buddy and Grandpa can make me feel. Uncle Buddy steps from around the building long enough to pull me back there with him.

"Uncle Buddy!" I crying out as my nose and eyes have a contest for which one can run the most water.

"Hush, child. Ain't no need to cry. I'm all right."

"But Uncle Buddy, where have you been?"

"Hiding, child. I'm hiding to stay alive."

"Oh Lord, Uncle Buddy, Grandpa is dead."

"I know, honey. I know. Harlem ain't nothing but home away from home for people from down South. I have known Papa was dead ever since the day he died."

"Oh, Uncle Buddy, I'm so sorry you couldn't come to the funeral."

"But I *was* there, my child."

"You were? Where?"

"The gravediggers. When someone dies don't nobody ever pay attention to the gravediggers. There were three men that were suppose to dig the grave. The Masons got me a uniform and a digging tool and I helped dig the hole for Daddy Braxton's finally resting place. When the undertaker asked the family to leave the cemetery, they opened the casket one last time so that I could say good-bye to him. It was raining so hard, folks didn't even notice who was who. Them so-called smart white folks was so sure I was going to try to come in with the pallbearers or the friends of the family that they never thought about the gravediggers. That is who I was that day. As soon as the funeral was over, the Masons got me out of town and back up here."

"But how did you get home from Harlem for the funeral?"

"The blue Cadillac, child. I rode with BarJean and Coy as far as Emporia, Virginia. From there a few of the Masons picked me up and I stayed down in the Low Meadows with Bro Smitty. Ain't no white folks coming down there. They ain't been down there since the flood of 1940 came and scared the mess out of them."

Oh, Lord, we hug and hug.

We cry and cry.

"They caught them, Uncle Buddy," I tell him. "The law caught the white men who tried to kill you."

"I know that too, child."

"Well, why are you still hiding? We can go home now."

"Child, I can't go back. They ain't going to send those men to jail and they ain't going to give me a fair trial because they think I tried to harm that white gal. Pattie Mae, I can't ever go back."

I don't say anything else. I just stand there and listen to my uncle Buddy tell me how he has been hiding ever since he left down home. How the good colored folks in Harlem have looked out for him. Especially Mr. Tom, who let him stay in his basement all this time.

"It's time for you to leave, child. Do not tell BarJean you saw me. She don't need to know where I am. She know I'm here somewhere and she know I'm all right. Now you go on and don't come back."

"No, Uncle Buddy, no. Please come with me."

"Don't you talk back to me, child. Get out of here."

His voice almost scares me. I hug him and walk away. But then I stop and go back to my uncle Buddy.

"Open your hand, Uncle."

He give me a look like he think I am going to put a worm in it like I did the last time I told him to open up.

I take one of Grandpa's obituaries from my pocket and put it in his hand.

"Bye, Uncle Buddy. Bye, Mr. Tom."

We wave good-bye to each other as Uncle Buddy disappears as fast as he had walked around that corner.

Lord, I feel ten pounds lighter now I know my uncle really is in Harlem. He really is alive!

I did not breathe a word about seeing Uncle Buddy to BarJean that afternoon. She was sitting in the kitchen waiting for me when I got back. I lied and told her I had just gone for a short walk.

She don't believe me. She ain't saying a word. Just looking at me. This means she is going to tell Ma as soon as she can get her on the phone. BarJean ain't much on fussing. She is good on tattling. Watch and see. Finally she is talking.

"You ready to go shopping?" she asks.

I say yes faster than I ever said it in my life.

BarJean changes into her walking shoes and out the door we go.

Our first stop is the fabric store, just like BarJean promised.

"Oh, Lord, BarJean, I ain't never seen so much fabric in my life."

"Pick five different colors for skirts. Coy said he will buy you some blouses later. And stop saying ain't in Harlem."

I want to scream, *ain't, ain't, ain't,* but Miss BarJean is really silly about this word mess now and I don't want to make her mad again. She might change her mind and we will not be here in the store shopping. I know what I will do. I will tell Uncle Buddy how she is acting.

I pick red, blue, white, brown, and light blue fabric for my skirts. BarJean walks over to the counter and gets the thread and she is talking to some black woman who works here.

"Come over here, Pattie Mae," BarJean calls to me. "I want to introduce you to Miss Sara."

Miss Sara. I'm walking slow. She don't just work here. This is her store. She own it. The sign out front says SARA'S FABRIC. Harlem sure is something. Wait till I tell Chick-A-Boo.

We talk to Miss Sara for a long time. Her and BarJean talk about everything under the sun except Uncle Buddy. People don't even mention his name. But when we leave, she hugs BarJean real tight and whispers something in her ear. You know these grown folks are going to force me to put a mason jar for ease dropping in my pocketbook and carry it everywhere I go.

"Hi, BarJean," a voice says from behind us.

"Hi, Mary," BarJean says as she turns around and hug this woman who know BarJean and don't know me.

BarJean introduce me to Miss Mary as my new sister-in-law. This is the girl Coy is going to marry. She sure is pretty and a Harlem girl. She is all dress up on a Saturday. She must really love Coy, because she just talking about him and that wedding. She got her arms filled with fabric that she say is for her wedding dress.

"It was nice to meet you, Miss Mary," I say, to let BarJean know I am sick of listening to grown folks business. We say our good-byes to Miss Sara and Miss Mary, pay for our stuff, and leave.

"Where we going now, BarJean?" I ask when we get out on the street.

"To the jewelry store."

"The jewelry store. What we going to do there?"

"I thought you wanted your ears pierced."

"Well, I do, but what about Ma?"

"Look, if we get your ears pierced now, they will be all healed with your birthstone in them by the time you get back to Rehobeth Road. Ma can't do nothing about it then but fuss."

BarJean don't know what she talking about. When Chick-A-Boo's oldest sister, Marniece, took a hot needle and a piece of thread and pierced her own ears, Miss Blanche made her take her earrings out and her holes closed right back up. Marniece got her ears pierced again when she went to Newport News to stay with her Aunt Lillian for the summer. When she got back they were already healed with her birthstone in them. Miss Blanche made her take her $2.00 earrings out and her holes closed right back up again. I'm not even going to tell BarJean about Marniece, because I want my holes in my ears. I will just have to take a chance on Ma killing me when I get back to Rehobeth Road.

"Have a seat right here, little lady," the girl in the jewelry store says after BarJean pays $1.00 for my ear piercing. "Now, hold still."

She rubs some alcohol on both my ears and then she taking out her own needle and thread. I can't believe it. I thought she was going to use one of them machines that Uncle Buddy told me his women folks got their ears pierced with. But she ain't. I'm all the way in Harlem getting my ears pierced with a needle and thread. I could have done this right on Rehobeth Road!

It hurts a little, but not too much.

I am just looking at myself in the mirror. My ears look good. Wait till Chick-A-Boo see me.

"Your ears look nice, little sister," BarJean says as I am still looking in the mirror.

"Thank you, sister. Are we going home now?"

"No, we still got to get your hair fixed. We suppose to be at Miss Van's Beauty Shop in twenty minutes."

BarJean and me run down the streets with all

my bags, just laughing like old times. Times before they took my uncle and grandpa from us.

Miss Van is a piece of work. She got fake hair, fake eyelashes, and clothes like the dancers I saw on the sign with Mr. Ellington at the Apollo Theater. I'm not going to ask if she owns this place because the sign outside says VAN'S BEAUTY PARLOR.

I ain't never seen so many women getting their hair fixed in one day before in my life. Those women are something else. I do not need a mason jar in here. They just talking their heads off.

Miss Van is not heating a straighten comb, so I do not know what she is going to do to my hair. I sho' hope she ain't going to braid it up.

A jar of perm! As she is pulling that jar of perm from under her counter, I feel faint again. Piece by piece she put perm in my hair after she covers my newly pressed ears. Miss Van laughs and says I do not need as much perm as BarJean because my hair ain't as nappy as hers.

When she finish my hair, she don't even put rubber bands on it. Miss Van is pulling my hair back with a piece of white ribbon to make a headband and my hair just fall on my shoulders like a real teenager. Like a real city girl.

Now we can go home.

Wait till Uncle Buddy see my pierced ears and my new hairdo.

10

Back South

*I*t's Monday morning and BarJean gone
back to work. I don't care what Uncle Buddy said.
I have to talk him into coming home with me.

I am sleepy because we were up all night
making my new clothes. BarJean is good with
that sewing machine. She let me cut out all the
patterns and she did the sewing. When she
finished, I put the buttons on the clothes. I am
going to be as clean as Willie Gatling when I
get back to Rich Square. That's what folks at
home say when you real dressed up. They do

not say you dressed up. They say, "You clean as Willie Gatling." You see, can't nobody get cleaner than Uncle Buddy's friend Willie Gatling. He is always dressed fine from head to toe. He gets cleaner than Uncle Buddy. I ain't never seen him without a suit. He works at the sawmill too and Uncle Buddy says he don't wear a tie to work, but he is always in a jacket.

I can't wear my new stuff today. I got walking to do. Back to the shoeshine stand I go.

Mr. Tom mad because I am back down here. But I tell him I'm going to keep coming until he tells Uncle Buddy to come back.

On the third day he said, "Come back tomorrow, child." I finally wore him down.

"I will be back early, okay?"

He don't even look up from shining some man's shoes.

"Mr. Tom, do Mr. Wright really live in Paris?"

"Yes, child, he do. He moved there last year. Times hard in the South, but they ain't easy here, either. They really ain't easy for a man like Mr. Wright."

"But why, Mr. Tom? You like it here. Why he any different than you?"

"You ask him when you see him again."

I will do just that, I'm thinking to myself as I walk away.

I'm at the shoeshine stand the next morning before Mr. Tom could get his rag box open.

There he is. There's Uncle Buddy.

"Hey, Uncle Buddy!" I yell and jump into his arms.

We just hugging, hugging, and hugging.

"Why, Pattie Mae, you got your ears pierced, and look at your hair."

"Yes, sir, I did."

"You look real pretty," he says.

I knew he would see my newly pierced ears and my new hairdo. That's how Uncle Buddy keeps his women folks happy. He notices everything about them.

He's laughing because he knows that sister of his is going to skin me alive when I get home.

Now it's time for the talking. Talking Uncle

Buddy into coming home. If I cry a little, surely he will come back with me.

"Come back to BarJean's apartment with me, Uncle Buddy. I want her to know that you all right. I hear her crying about you late, late at night."

He sits there for a few moments and then he says no. When he says no, I just cross my legs and do what Chick-A-Boo told me to do if I ever need to for an important reason. Lie!

"Uncle Buddy, Grandma don't look right. She is gray in the face and I think she might die, too. Her heart is broke, just like Grandpa's."

A tear rolls down Uncle Buddy's cheek.

"Uncle Buddy, I believe if Grandma can just see you once more she will be all right."

"Lord, Pattie Mae, you probably right. This mess done killed the only daddy I ever had. I cannot let it kill Ma Babe too."

Well! He does not say so, but I know we going back to Rehobeth Road on the first train leaving Harlem.

He put his hat and dark glasses on and we walk the back streets of Harlem all the way to BarJean's.

It ain't but twelve o'clock, so we just sit in the living room and talk. Finally the front door open.

BarJean eyes get just as big as fifty-cent piece and down she goes. The girl done fainted. I don't know why she fainted. She knew good and well Uncle Buddy was up here somewhere. When she wake up, me and Uncle Buddy is standing over her while she rest in the bed where he put her.

"Uncle Buddy, is it really you?"

"It's me, child, it's me."

"What you doing here with Pattie Mae?"

"Well, I told you that she is the smartest one in the bunch. She came and found me when all of Rich Square and Harlem couldn't."

They hug and hug.

It's a few days later and Uncle Buddy announces that we are going back home tomorrow. Grandpa ain't there, but it's still home. BarJean ain't coming with us because she got to work. My aunts are back in Harlem now and me and Uncle Buddy done been to see them and Coy, too. Collie was not home when we went to Aunt Louise's, thank the Lord.

All our folks are trying to tell Uncle Buddy not to go home. But he told them he got to see Ma Babe for himself. Coy, he ain't saying nothing. He don't even tell Uncle Buddy that Ma Babe is okay. He looking kind of strange. It's probably because Ma and her sisters yelled at the poor man the entire time he was trying to drive them around to take care of grown folks business about Grandpa's will.

Before we leave, I go by the shoeshine and say good-bye to Mr. Tom. Just my luck, Mr. Wright is getting his shoes shined.

Mr. Tom had told him all about Uncle Buddy, and Mr. Wright was concerned about us. I thought that was mighty nice. Mr. Wright talks to me for about two hours about what to do and not to do when I get back home. That man got a whole lot of sense.

"You know, Pattie Mae, when I was a little boy living down South, I lived in a house on an old plantation, just like Tom told me you do now. It was called Rucker's Plantation. My daddy, Nathaniel, was a sharecropper and my mother was a schoolteacher. She taught me well, but my daddy left us, just like your daddy left. Left us for another woman. Those were hard times. Finally we moved in with my aunt and uncle Silas Hopkins."

I can't believe my ears. Silas is my daddy's name.

Mr. Wright keeps on talking.

"One night some white men came to our house in the middle of the night and killed my uncle because he was a black man with money. He owned his own salon and made lots and lots of money. That did not sit well with the white folks. It scared Mother and my aunt so bad that we left for Chicago after the funeral. From Chicago I moved to New York. As a writer it's been hard here, so I moved to Paris. I moved to Paris for the same reason Tom don't go south of Baltimore. I moved there to be respected as a black man. I'll be leaving again soon because that is where I can survive as a man, as a writer. That's what your uncle and Tom trying to do. They are trying to survive as black men. Remember that."

He just talking and talking. I like Mr. Wright. I like what he saying. I mainly like the way he never use the word colored or Negro when he is talking.

"This is for you, Pattie Mae," Mr. Wright says.

It's a book!

Native Son by Mr. Richard Wright.

"Thank you, Mr. Wright."

I place the book careful in my pocketbook and take a bag Mr. Tom gives me. It is a box of cigarettes for Mr. Charlie and some hatpins for Miss Doleebuck. These will look good in her nice Sunday hats.

I am on my way. It is time to go home. Home to Rehobeth Road. Home to Grandma. BarJean and Coy give us a ride to the train station. She just crying because we are leaving. I will miss her, but that crying? Oh, no.

On the train home, me and Uncle Buddy just talking about everything under the sun.

"Uncle Buddy, do you think they going to put you in jail again?"

"Child, who knows with white folks? But what I do know is I ain't going to stay down South when this trial is over."

That's not what I want to hear, but I don't want to say nothing right now. So I just shut my mouth.

Our train ride home is as sweet as bee honey. Uncle Buddy only leave his seat to go to the bathroom because he does not want white folks to see him. They definitely will not run into him in a "colored only" bathroom. According to Bay Boy, some of the crazy white folks at home talking about they want to bring Uncle Buddy back to Rich Square dead or alive. No matter what they saying, Uncle Buddy did not do anything wrong and it's time for the truth to come out. Crazy white folks.

I know when we are in North Carolina because even in the twilight, through the train window, I can see nothing but white. White cotton. If you ain't never seen cotton grow, you have really missed something special.

When I left, the cotton was barely out of the bow. Now it's everywhere. Look-a-here, I'm not picking one piece of cotton this year! I am a city girl now. Besides, I talked Uncle Buddy into coming home when no one else could. So it's my job to stay close to him, close to home. So no cotton picking for me.

The train done stopped in Rocky Mount and I can see Ma standing there in a dress that I have never seen before. I'm sure that one of her sisters gave it to her because Ma don't buy many new clothes. Ma got the law and Mr. Charlie with her. Ma already told Uncle Buddy on the telephone that the law is taking him into custody for his own protection after they take him by Jones Property to see Grandma. Protection! They got some nerve. That is how this whole mess got started in the first place. If they had been protecting Uncle Buddy, he would not have been in trouble. I step off the train first and walk up to Ma.

"Don't cry, Ma, it's going to be okay."

She hugs me with one arm and Uncle Buddy with the other. Then we all get in Mr. Charlie's car and head home with Sheriff Franklin following us back to Rich Square. Back to Jones Property. There are three more cars behind Sheriff Franklin and it ain't the Klan. Mr. Charlie says he told the black Masons to come too. They didn't get out of their cars, but as soon as we pull out of the train station, they pull out right behind us. Mr.

Charlie wait until we are on the road to tell us about the Masons. After that, nobody is saying a word all the way to Rich Square.

Lord, turning on Rehobeth Road is really hurting my heart. I don't know life here without my grandpa. Mr. Charlie just drove right past our house and I know we are going to Jones Property first. There's Grandma with Miss Doleebuck and Mr. George. They sitting in the screened-in porch so that the flies and mosquitoes don't get them. Grandma done stood up and she walking off the porch. The same porch where my grandpa used to sit every night. The one he built with his own hands.

"Lord, I want to thank you for bringing my child home," Grandma crying into the night air.

"Yes, Lord," Miss Doleebuck cries out. Mr. George just sitting here crying away. He ain't shouted or cried a tear since Mr. Perry and Mr. Massey died. He must be thinking about his own boys.

Uncle Buddy is getting out of the car mighty slow. I think he wants to go back to Harlem before the women start shouting for real.

Too late. They shouting to beat the band. So Uncle Buddy just picks Grandma up and he is swinging her around like she ain't got no bones in her body. I'm just standing looking at them. Uncle Buddy didn't think he would ever see her again. Grandma didn't think she would ever see him either.

"Your daddy gone on, son. Lord, I wish he would have lived to see you one more time."

That is the beginning of them talking. Uncle Buddy does not ask Grandma about being sick. I reckon he knew I lied the minute he saw Grandma wasn't turning gray. Uncle Buddy would have lied to save the Jones family too. So he just keep on talking. He tells her all about being a gravedigger at the funeral. They talk for an hour. Until the sheriff, who is sitting in his car, says, "Time to go."

Now that it's time for Uncle Buddy to leave, the shouting has started all over again.

"Don't cry, Ma Babe, it's going to be all right," Uncle Buddy says as he climbing into Sheriff Franklin's car.

Uncle Buddy rode here with us, but the sheriff says he got to ride back with them and that's final. But it ain't nothing the sheriff can do about all them Masons following them to wherever they taking my uncle. They are lining up like they going to a funeral and when Sheriff Franklin pulls out, they follow him. They done made up their minds that they ain't letting Uncle Buddy out of their sight. Even Mr. Charlie goes. Mr. George stays behind with us women folks. As soon as the dust settles from all these cars leaving Jones Property, I'm going to ask Ma where they taking Uncle Buddy.

They gone.

Now we all just sitting here looking at each other, so this is a good time for me to ask.

"Ma, can I ask a grown folks question?"

She just looks at me. I don't know how old I have to be to know what is going on in the world. Right now I will settle for what is going on right here on Rehobeth Road. Maybe after I tell her that I met Richard Wright she will know I know some grown folks stuff.

"Ma, where they taking my uncle Buddy?"

"Honey, they taking your uncle up to Raleigh to the State Correction Center. He ain't under arrest, they just taking him there for safekeeping."

I don't say a word. Because grown folks think that I'm crazy. I already heard Coy tell BarJean what the law did to the seven white men that tried to hang Uncle Buddy. Nothing! They didn't do nothing to them. They didn't even go to their houses to arrest them. When the law realized that the white men had not killed Uncle Buddy, word got around and the next thing you know, Coy said, papers all over the state were writing about what happened to Uncle Buddy. That is the only reason that Sheriff Franklin arrested those men. He just sent word to each one of them to come to his house. He didn't even handcuff them. He told them they were under arrest and then had white men from all over the county waiting in his living room to post their bail. Even Mayor Smith was there and helped with the bail. It was graduation day for the schoolchildren, and the superintendent for Northampton County left graduation to help post the bail. What kind of mess is that? Them white men folks were back out on the street before suppertime.

I just can't wait to see what kind of trial they give Uncle Buddy. I just want to see how they treat them white folks and how they treat my uncle. Accordingly to what I hear Coy tell BarJean, they going to have their trial on the same day. That ain't right either. I hate going to bed mad, but I'm mad as one of Mr. Bay's bulls tonight.

Two weeks passed before they announced Uncle Buddy's trial date.

11

The Courthouse

I didn't sleep much last night. Uncle Buddy's trial is going to start in two hours and I just want it to be over with. I want the judge to tell them seven white men that they was wrong for what they done to my uncle. I want them to know that they killed my grandpa. We will see in a little while.

Not a word is being said on Jones Property this morning. Everyone just dressing and praying to they self. I know they praying because they lips just moving and ain't nothing coming out.

Mr. Charlie don't suppose to be driving but here he come. He get out and come inside.

"Mornin', Babe."

"Mornin', Charlie. We're ready."

Without saying another word, we all go onto the back porch, then head for Mr. Charlie's car. Miss Doleebuck inside the car waiting for us and yes, she is all dressed in black with one of her famous wide hats on.

"Mornin', Miss Doleebuck," I say.

"Good morning, child."

Those are the last words said from Jones Property all the way to the courthouse in Jackson.

We just riding around and riding around because it ain't no place to park near the courthouse. There must be something else going on in downtown Jackson today. It looks like Harlem, it's so many cars parked on the streets.

Walking up the courthouse steps, I can see people I know real good already going inside. Miss Nora, Mr. Bay, Miss Blanche, Miss Novella; even Ole Man Taylor is here. I can't believe my eyes when we get inside. This courthouse is full to the top. No wonder it ain't nowhere to park. No black folks are picking cotton today because they are all right here. And white folks ain't doing whatever white folks do all day either because they are all here too.

The black folks side of the courthouse is full already. Mr. William Spencer Creecy, the schoolhouse principal, just spotted us and he motioning with his big hands for us to come down front.

"Good morning to you all," he says in his big, strong voice as he points to an empty row.

"I saved seats for you, Miss Babe. For you and your family."

I smile at Mr. Creecy because I don't know anybody on this earth like him. He is the only man I know other than Uncle Buddy that I can speak his name in the same breath with my grandpa. Well, maybe Mr. Wright. But Mr. Creecy got something that even my grandpa didn't have. He got schooling. A lot of schooling. He went to Shaw University a few years and graduated from Elizabeth City College. He is the reason I want to go to Shaw. I want to talk like he talks. I want to stand straight and proud like him. Mr. Creecy can make white folks do anything.

Word around town is Mr. Creecy gave Mayor Smith a tongue-lashing for helping bail them seven men out of jail who tried to hang Uncle Buddy. Yep, it's safe to say that white folks scared of Mr. Creecy. He got something hanging in his office that they are never going to have in their nice white houses. A college degree!

"Mercy to the highest," I say when I look behind us.

"What is it, child?" Ma asks as I turn around and look in the back of the courthouse again.

"Look, Ma, the black folks done started sitting on the white folks' side. It ain't enough room for them over here."

Up until ten minutes before the trial starts, that's what they do. They come in and sit right beside the white folks. Fed up is what black folks are. They are fed up! They going to sit where they want to sit this day.

"All rise," Sheriff Franklin, who is the sheriff

over here in Jackson, says as the judge coming in. That's the same judge who moved Uncle Buddy's court date from June to November, giving them white boys time to break Uncle Buddy out of jail and try to hang him. I know this ain't nice, but I just want to run up there and slap the taste out of that judge's mouth. He is mad as all get-up. Ma says he mad because of all the reporters that are going to write about this God forsaken place when this trial is over. He mad because he can't hide what is really going on around here no more!

The judge takes his seat, and then we all set down. The lawyer who says he represents them white men stands up and starts talking the craziest mess I have heard since they arrested my uncle. I can't believe what I am hearing. Now, I ain't but twelve going on thirteen, but I do know that this ain't the way no trial is suppose to be. The lawyer is making speeches about what the South suppose to be like, talking about Southern tradition, and the heritage of white folks, and how pure the white woman is. Now he talking about the horror of Reconstruction. Well, thank God Mr. Wright told me what Reconstruction means and how it's a good thing. Well, good for black folks and bad for white folks.

According to Mr. Wright, after slavery ended white folks was killing colored folks just because they were not slaves anymore. But then things kind of settled down for a minute and before you knew it, whites was living in their world and colored were living in theirs. Somehow white folks just thought black folks were getting too big for our britches and they started all this lynching, just like they did right after President Lincoln freed the slaves in 1863.

Mr. Wright said one way the white men justified killing colored men was they claimed that the black men were raping white women. Maybe a few black men were doing bad stuff, but Mr. Wright said it was no different than all the bad stuff the white man had done to black folks for three hundred years. Three hundred years. Lord, that is a long time for people to be treated like dogs. Mr. Wright told me the reason my skin is as light as it is, is because of white men raping black women. I believe him too, because he showed me some pictures of some real Africans and they were black-black and blue-black. Mr. Wright and me both agree that is the color we all should be.

So I sit here and listen to the white attorney for the seven white men who tried to kill my uncle talk all that crazy mess. But I know better.

I'm holding on to a new pocketbook that I bought in Harlem. Ain't much money in it. But I got Mr. Wright's book and Grandpa's obituary in here. I gave one obituary to Uncle Buddy and got me another one out of the chest when I got back to Rehobeth Road. This is for me, for life. I wanted to bring something that would make these white folks straighten up and act right. Maybe they will feel Grandpa here like I do today. They should feel his presence because they killed him and this obituary is proof.

My grandpa was a good man. He would have liked Mr. Wright and all the stuff he told me about the North and the South. Grandpa liked hearing the truth.

Yeah, I'm glad that I got my hair permed for the first time in my life. I like the clothes BarJean made for me and the blouses Coy bought for me and most of all just to have the sight of Harlem in my head is real nice. But I learned about black folks and our heritage in Harlem. I like knowing the truth about freedom. I know that we were not always slaves and sharecroppers. I know that there were men before my grandpa that owned their own land. We ain't animals like I hear Ole Man Taylor call Miss Blanche's boy, Felix, one day. We are from Africa. Our grandfolks were kings and queens. That's what Mr. Wright said, and I believe him. Now this white man standing up here trying to tell me who we are.

Finally the lawyer is finished lying and now he is talking about why we are really here. He still making me sick talking about Uncle Buddy tried to rape that white woman and his clients being here because they are falsely accused of breaking into the county jail with the intent to hang Uncle Buddy. He just talking away until the judge ask for a recess.

"What is he talking about recess, Ma? Uncle Buddy lawyer ain't talked yet."

"Don't know, child. Let's just get something to eat and come back."

"I ain't hungry, Ma. Can I just sit outside and wait for you?"

"You can, as long as you stay in one spot."

I follow Ma and Grandma outside. I set outside long enough for Ma to get across the street with Grandma to the black section of Jackie's Cafeteria. I can't wait to get back in that courthouse to see why we have to take a recess at eleven o'clock in the morning. Maybe Ma didn't notice, but I noticed that most of the white folks didn't move from their seats.

Ain't nobody paying me no attention while I'm walking back up these big cement stairs. Nobody paying me one bit of attention peeking inside the courtroom either. They don't have time for me. They are having some kind of celebration. But for what?

Oh, Lord! This is worse than trying to hang Uncle Buddy. They got a big picture of that man, Matt Ransom, and they getting ready to hang it over the judge's bench. Now, Matt Ransom ain't never done nothing bad to me, but he ain't no hero to black folks. Grandpa use to tell me about that man all the time. He said that when the Yankees came to Northampton County to free slaves, Matt Ransom and his soldiers met them at the county line and turned hundreds of Yankees away. A few got through and did some damage to the plantations and tried to help slaves, but for the most part Matt Ransom led the charge that kept black folks in their place in this county long after slavery was over.

Now, here on the same day of my uncle Buddy's trial, they are hanging Matt Ransom's picture in the courthouse. This is the damndest thing I have ever seen. That's right, I cursed. And I will do it again. On top of that, the seven men who tried to hang Uncle Buddy are walking around at this reception like they something special. The other white folks are patting them on their back like they believe they did the right thing. This mess is too much for me. I am going back outside and I ain't telling no black folks what I just saw. Just as I turn to go out, I open my pocketbook to get a penny for a piece of bubble gum and Grandpa's obituary gets caught up in the wind from the door and blows right out of my hand. Up into the air, over them white men's heads and right on the face of Matt Ransom. It sits there for a minute. Then it falls between the wall and the judge's chair.

Grandpa is really here! He's here! Grandpa is trying to tell us everything is going to be all right.

I run over to Kennedy's Dime Store for my bubble gum.

After the so-called recess, all the black folks come back inside and now everyone is whispering about the picture hanging behind the judge that was not there before. Most of them don't know who Matt Ransom is. But I know and if Grandpa was here, he would know. They also don't know that Grandpa's obituary flew right against that picture ten minutes ago. Something strange is about to happen. You just watch.

Sure enough, five minutes after the recess the judge makes his decision. All seven men are acquitted. Mr. Wright told me what the word acquit means after I told him we were coming back down South for the trial. He said that acquittal means the white men were not going to stand trial and the case was over. Uncle Buddy said the word acquit means "white folks don't get punished for trying to hang a nigger." I think it means a little of both.

White folks just jumping up and down like they won some money. Colored folks ain't saying a word. Grandma just hanging her head.

The judge finally asks everyone to sit down and it look like they are going to start Uncle Buddy's trial now. At least we thought they were. Within a minute the judge tells the court that Uncle Buddy is acquitted too. They all crazy! The only reason they letting Uncle Buddy go is they do not want to tell the truth. They do not want to bring that white woman out here and let her tell the truth that Uncle Buddy ain't never tried to touch her lily-white skin.

Black folks cheering now. As happy as I am for Uncle Buddy, I ain't cheering. I ain't cheering because this is what Mr. Wright said they were going to do. He said they were going to let them white folks go free and Uncle Buddy, too, so that the news reporters will leave town. Some of the reporters were already gone. Chick-A-Boo told me that there was a white reporter here last month all the way from the London *Times*. That's right, from London, England. He left because some of the local whites told him that he was going to find himself in the Roanoke River if he stayed. The Roanoke River is one scary river. It's back there in Occoneechee Neck. Let me tell you something. That white reporter don't want to end up in there. Scared the man so bad that he left and said he was never coming back. He said Rich Square was evil, and I agree with that. All of the reporters did not leave. Uncle Buddy mostly talks with the black reporters when we get outside. One white reporter asks, "Well, Goodwin, what are you going to do now?"

"I'm leaving as soon as I go by the old home place to get my suitcase."

When the white reporter walks away, Uncle Buddy tells the black newspaper people that he is going to stay on Jones Property tonight and leave for Harlem in a few days. He know better than to tell them white folks the truth. If they thought Uncle Buddy was going to stay with us tonight, they would try to hang all of us right there on Jones Property. Probably under the old oak tree that the tornado didn't blow down.

12

The Storm

The telephone is ringing before we can even get out of the bed at Grandma's this morning. I can tell from the way Ma is talking and saying big words that it is Lawyer Jenkins, Uncle Buddy's lawyer. I grab my mason jar so I can hear better.

She is off the telephone now and going into the kitchen to tell Grandma and Uncle Buddy what the lawyer said. There must be some good white folks in the world after all. According to Ma, Governor Cherry of North Carolina is asking for a new trial. Not just a new trial, but he taking this mess over to Warren County to the big courthouse. They have what Ma says is the Superior Court there, where people go when they do not get the right verdict over in Jackson. Ma says that the governor said for Uncle Buddy to come back to Jones Property if he has left. Of course the governor's white too, so he don't know that Uncle Buddy sitting right here at the kitchen table. He don't need to know that.

White folks mad as all get-up with the governor. I been reading in the paper that he receives ugly letters from white folks every day. According to Miss Mannie, who cleans up for Sheriff Franklin, the sheriff's wife wrote the governor and told him a piece of her mind. So did most of the white women in Rich Square. White folks do not want any part of this mess. They just want it to go away like water that disappears on a hot summer day.

Even Mr. J. Edgar Hoover, the director of the FBI, was involved for two minutes. That's how this mess became big, big news. Governor Cherry contacted the FBI and asked them to investigate when Uncle Buddy first left. Mr. Hoover didn't care about us. He sent the FBI down here only to close his investigation in a day and he told the newspapers, "No federal law has been broken." But the law is the law and he should be shame of himself. Lord knows he ought to be shame of himself. And our so-called mayor should be ashamed too. He told the white newspapermen, "We like our coloreds as long as they stay in their place."

I don't know where our place is. All I know is this is the biggest mess since Ole Man Taylor caught his wife in bed with Mr. Stanley, who use to be the overseer for the land on Rehobeth Road. I was a baby then, but I heard that Ole Man Taylor said he was going to kill Mr. Stanley, but he didn't. He didn't have to. See, another mess happen right after that. Mr. Stanley was fussing with his main field hand Johnnie Lucas about some receipts that Johnnie brought to Mr. Stanley for some cotton he had picked. Mr. Stanley gave Johnnie $8.00 and Johnnie said the first receipt was for $10.00. Ma was in the field when it happen. She said that before they could do anything about it, Johnnie had grabbed an ice pick from the back of Mr. Stanley's black Chevy and stabbed Mr. Stanley to death. Ma said Johnnie ran and somehow made it North. There was a reward put out for Johnnie and some white folks turned him in. They brought Johnnie back here and took him up to the state prison in Raleigh and he got the electric chair. Now they want us to believe that they had Uncle Buddy there for safekeeping.

All kind of stuff happened around this place long before I was born. My grandpa said that when he was a little boy they hung a man, Jeter Mitchell, right in front of the courthouse where we were yesterday. Black folks believe Mr. Jeter did nothing wrong, just like Uncle Buddy didn't do nothing. But white folks claim Mr. Jeter raped a white woman over in Occoneechee Neck. He was arrested, just like Uncle Buddy, and they took him out of jail in the middle of the night, just like Uncle Buddy. Sure enough, they hung him right on the tree that is still standing here.

Grandpa said didn't nobody try to help that poor soul. Even if Mr. Jeter did what the white folks said he did, they did not have to hang the man. They should have gave him a trial like they give white men who rape women. Now that I think about it, I think I ain't never sitting under that tree again. Never!

After Ma finish telling Uncle Buddy and Grandma what the attorney said, Uncle Buddy say he will not stay here until the second trial. He say it ain't going to do a bit of good. He is ready to go back to Harlem. Back to a place where a man can be a man.

The next morning me and Uncle Buddy get up early. We have not said a word to nobody on Jones Property, but our plan is to go to Grandpa's grave today.

"Morning, Ma Babe," Uncle Buddy says to Grandma while she snapping green peas on the back porch.

"Mornin', son. What you doing up so early and why you so dressed up?"

"I thought I would take Pattie Mae and go pay my respects to Pa this morning. You and Mer want to ride with us?"

"Boy, you all go on. I am going to help Mer pack up her things today. They moving back down the road to their house today. You know she ain't stayed home a good two nights since you was arrested."

Ma comes out on the porch. "Yes, bro, it's time for me and Pattie Mae to go home."

I wish that woman would speak for herself. I do not want to go back to that slave house. Grandpa is dead and we should stay right here with Grandma and Uncle Buddy. But you can't tell that woman nothing.

"I'm ready, Uncle Buddy," I say, rushing past Ma and Grandma with Hobo running behind me. He jumps on the back of the truck as we ride off. Hudson don't want to come. He just looking at us. That's a smart cat. I swear he know where we going.

All the way to the graveyard we laugh and talk just like old times. But when we turning down that long path to where Grandpa's grave is, Uncle Buddy ain't talking no more.

"You all right, Uncle Buddy?"

"I'm fine, child. What about you?"

"I'm fine too."

It rained last night and it's muddy so we parking back a ways and I guess we are going to walk the rest of the way. Uncle Buddy helps me out of the truck the way he says a gentleman is suppose to help a lady. I'm telling you, Uncle Buddy is good with the women folks.

This is my first time walking past all these graves without being out here for a funeral.

"Look, Uncle Buddy, this is June Bug's grave." We stop and say a prayer. When I open my eyes, I look around me and realize that me and Uncle Buddy are standing in the middle of our whole family. All the Lewises, all the Joneses, and a few folks that ain't got none of our blood.

Uncle Buddy starting to walk slower and slower when he gets closer to Grandpa's grave. I'm going to stop here and let him walk on by himself. Hobo got good sense too, because he stops walking when I stop. Grandpa said that some doors a man has to walk through by his self. Poor Uncle Buddy.

He just standing there. I ain't never seen him cry before. He gets all down on his knees just crying and praying over Grandpa's grave.

"Oh, Pa," he says, "I want to thank you for being my daddy. I want to thank you for taking me in when my folks died and all. Pa, I know you died from a broken heart and I am sorry about that. I am sorry I ran off and left you here to deal with the white folks all by yourself. You know, Pa, everything about being a man that I know, you taught me. Pa, will you forgive me for not being here when you took your last breath? Please forgive me, Pa."

No sooner than Uncle Buddy said them words, it thundered. It thundered loud. I'm usually scared to death of a storm, but not today. I know in my heart that's Grandpa talking back to Uncle Buddy. So I just walk over to Uncle Buddy and put my hand on his shoulder. Hobo let out a howl louder than I have ever heard him make.

"Grandpa's all right, Uncle Buddy. It's time to go home."

He stand up and we start to walk away. Then he stop.

"Wait, Pattie Mae. I got one more thing to do here."

He turns around and takes something out of his coat pocket. It is a framed picture. Not just any picture. It is the obituary of Grandpa's ma, Mary Lee Jones, with a flower framed in it. He puts it on Grandpa's grave.

"Now, Pa, you got some company. You always been here for us and we don't want to leave you here all by yourself. I found it in the old chest in the living room. I hope you like it."

We go home.

All seems quiet on Rehobeth Road until Uncle Buddy announces that he is leaving. Leaving for Harlem. He says he love us, but he ain't never coming back to Jones Property. Said he ain't never coming back south of Baltimore.

Author's Note

When I was a little girl growing up on Rehobeth Road in Rich Square, North Carolina, my grandmother, Babe Jones, told me the story of Buddy Bush. Her version was:

"White folks said that boy Buddy tried to rape a white woman out in town. Colored folks said it ain't so, but the law got after Buddy Bush and we ain't never see him no more."

That was her story, and that was what she said until the day she died. It was her truth, and my truth was that I wanted to write her story. I wanted to one day tell the story of Buddy Bush, the legend of Buddy Bush.

I also wanted people to know who Babe and Braxton Jones were. I wanted the world to know where Rehobeth Road is located and about all the good folks who walked up and down that road in the hot sun to see one another. They walked to

Jones Property to see how Miss Babe and Mr. Braxton were doing. When nighttime came, they sat on the front porch while Grandma held court. They listened. I listened. Listening to Grandma gave me a voice to tell the world about "the incident" that changed a town. "The incident" that people are still talking about fifty years later.

When *The Legend of Buddy Bush* was published, it did exactly what my grandma always did; it fascinated people. At every turn, strangers questioned me about Buddy Bush and his legend. They wanted to know what was true and what was fiction. People wanted to know where Rehobeth Road is. They wanted to know if Rich Square is a real place. When I told them "yes"—it was all real, with a little fiction for excitement—they asked the big question: Where is Buddy Bush?

That is when I realized that my work was not finished. I had to write *The Return of Buddy Bush* for my readers. People needed to know what my grandmother had not told me. I started to research the life of Buddy Bush and the court case surrounding "the incident." What my grandma said—and what I wrote in *The Legend of Buddy Bush*—about Buddy Bush getting away from the Klan was true, but his family did see him again.

Readers need to know that Buddy Bush came back to Rich Square, North Carolina, and was taken to the Raleigh Correction Prison for safekeeping until his trial. After one trial he was acquitted, and so were the seven men who tried to kill Buddy Bush. Governor Cherry was outraged and called for a second trial for three of the seven men, which was held in Warren County, but it only brought about a second acquittal. The ordeal was over. Buddy Bush left that courthouse and disappeared from the lives of the people who loved him forever.

In this sequel, readers travel with Pattie Mae to find Uncle Buddy and bring him home. Home to Jones Property. Home to where he belongs.

Court meets pursuant to a recess on Tuesday Morning, Aug. 5, 1947 at 9:30 O'clock A. M.

Minutes of Monday August 4, 1947 are read and approved and the following proceedings are had:

State

No. 728   Vs   Assault with intent to commit rape   NOt A True Bill

Godwin Bush alias Buddy Bush

S. G. Baugham
Foreman Grand Jury

State

No. 729   Vs   Conspiracy to B. & E. Jail to   NOT A TRUE BILL
                       Kill and Injure
Joe Lee Cunningham
Robert Vann   S. G. Baugham
Linwood Bryant   Foreman Grand Jury
W. C. Cooper
Glenn Collier
Gilbert Bryant
Russell Bryant

State

No. 729A   Vs   Breaking and entering with intent
                       to kill and injure   NOT A TRUE BILL
Joe Lee Cunningham
Robert Vann
Linwood Bryant   S. G. Baugham
W. C. Cooper   FOREMAN GRAND JURY
Glenn Collier
Gilbert Bryant
Russell Bryant

State

No. 729 B. Vs.   Kidnapping   NOT A TRUE BILL

Joe Lee Cunningham
Robert Vann   S. G. Baugham
Linwood Bryant   FOREMAN GRAND JURY
W. C. Cooper
Glenn Collier
Gilbert Bryant
Russell Bryant

Court documents from Buddy Bush's trial

Jones Property on Rehobeth Road

The inspiration for Mer Sheals
(the author's mother, Maless Moses),
around 1965 at the Slave House

Buddy Bush at his trial in Northampton County
Courthouse, Jackson, North Carolina